D1438704

A DIFFERENT FACE

Olivia Manning

A DIFFERENT FACE

Heinemann : London

William Heinemann Ltd
15 Queen Street, Mayfair, London W1X 8BE

LONDON MELBOURNE TORONTO
JOHANNESBURG AUCKLAND

First published 1953
Re-issued 1975

SBN 434 44909 1

To my Husband,
R. D. SMITH

Printed in Great Britain by
REDWOOD BURN LIMITED
Trowbridge & Esher

CHAPTER I

HUGO FLETCHER had scarcely drawn a breath of Coldmouth air when he asked himself what had brought him back here. He had been abroad twelve years. Time had softened memory, of course. Now, standing at the entrance to the harbour railway station, he recalled every sight, sound and smell of this murderous city.

And he had come straight here. Unnecessarily. He had planned to break his journey in London, but when he got off the Liverpool train and found himself, amidst a clamour of traffic, in foggy air smelling of old fish-boxes, pressed under a grey, glass roof as under a diving-bell, he was assailed by his old sense of being lost in the world. His one thought was to get away; and he had, after all, somewhere to go. He could go straight to Ridley School. There he would be, if nothing else, a man with a name, references in order and a position bought and paid for. Lured by security, he ran down the moving-staircase to the Tube, and, crossing under ground to another station, managed to get away with no more sight of London than the rail-side house-backs, ochre-coloured and blurred by autumnal fog.

He had, in fact, behaved like a fool. He was no longer poor. He could have faced London.

Now he had to face Coldmouth. There was no fog here. The air was sharp. The light from the ice-white sky gave an edge to the harbour's chill and choppy waters. On the other side of the Harbour Row was the dockyard wall. Round its seaward end appeared the great, grey stern of the battleship lying at the main dockyard berth. An identical ship had been lying there twelve years before when Hugo made his get-away and, for all the change in the scene, the same ship might have been lying there ever since. There were gaps in the famous row of harbour public-houses, but the dockyard wall still swept away in its long, unbroken curve to Old Coldmouth. Everything else in sight had a look of post-war exhaustion and shabbiness, but within the wall the buildings were intact and newly-painted. The main gate caught the eye, gold-leaf buttered thick on its ornamentations. No doubt it would all have magnificence for a stranger, but in Hugo it roused only an old resentment. His father had been in the Navy. He knew that in Coldmouth respect was not for the naval families cheeseparing on low pay, and less for the widows with their mouse-meal pensions, but for the business-men who ran the city in their own interests and each year bought a bigger car, or a bigger house, and took it in turns to become mayor.

He was angry again as he had been in adolescence and, irritated by his own anger, he strode down the station steps and joined a bus queue. Some moments passed before he realised his mistake. This queue was for the bus that would have taken him to Old Coldmouth. That was not where he was going. He may have been a fool to return here, but he was not such a fool as to return to his home. He had come back to lead an entirely different life—a life that would be like putting his foot upon the neck of his past in this place.

As he was about to cross the road and catch a bus going in the opposite direction, he remembered that Charles Martyn had had no warning of his arrival. Hugo's last letter, written from Port Said, had told of his intention of staying in London for two weeks. From there he was to write again.

He would have to return to the station and telephone the school.

Martyn, the headmaster, answered the telephone himself.

"This is Hugo Fletcher speaking. I must apologise for turning up like this, without warning. I couldn't face London just yet, so I came straight down."

The complete silence that followed Hugo's pause caused him to add: "Mustn't expect to land on you, of course. I'll look round for somewhere to stay."

"Certainly not." The headmaster's abruptness might have been nervousness. "Come straight here. We shall be delighted," but it would have been difficult to express less delight. "Expect you in about fifteen minutes." Martyn ended the conversation before Hugo had time to protest again.

Hugo went back to the bus stop. There had been no mention of sending a car for him—and surely the school had a car! Martyn's voice, repeating itself in his head, became for Hugo the voice of a man doing his duty distastefully. His vanity winced at it, and he had to remind himself that the headmaster had never seen him. But, supposing someone had already dragged up the story of the accident!

"Oh, to hell!" he said. "They've taken my money."

The matter went out of his mind when the bus swung out

of the harbour area into the city's bombed centre. The office blocks stood gutted and roofless. Of the main shopping centre to which, as a child, he had gone with his mother to look at the Christmas toy shows, there remained nothing but basements filled with young trees. The surrounding district had been so levelled the roads netted it like paths in a desert. This complete devastation struck at him like a blow. This was the only part of Coldmouth that had meant anything to him. When he had known he would return here, he had been possessed suddenly by a picture of himself, secure, well-dressed, a notable person, walking here on a sunny morning. It had given him a spasm of pure satisfaction. Every corner of this district had stood intact in his mind for twelve years, while, in fact, during most of that time there had been nothing. Nothing at all. He told himself angrily it would be these streets—streets just outside the range of the dockyard barrage—that had to suffer most. And it was somewhere here, in the midst of all this, that his mother had been killed.

Making its way southwards to the sea, the bus swung, first right, then left, and came out to the bright, grey esplanade. This was advertised as the longest esplanade on the south coast. Hugo had seen none of the others but he was certain this was also the most hideous. The tall, shore-facing houses, once all of red and corbelled sandstone, had been added to, refaced and, here and there, pulled down and replaced by Edwardian hotels and restaurants, by blocks of flats, in steel and glass, so that all the buildings of the front were as various as underwear on a line. There was even— Hugo watched out for it—a café in Babylonian style that, in childhood, had seemed to him sinister and now seemed

4

monstrous. His early dislike of the esplanade had been vague and half-guilty—he was not quite sure then that it was the esplanade and not he that was in the wrong—now he could admit a defined disapproval.

"Hideous," he said at it, "hideous!"

The promenade, chequered with great paving stones alternately pink and grey, stretched almost to vanishing point. In the distance, beyond the last bus stop, like a cloud against the sky, was the first rise of the cliffs.

The shore parallel with the promenade was a chill-coloured shingle over which the in and out of the sea slapped like a wet floorcloth. It was a deplorable beach in the best of weather and the municipality had tried to hide it with ornamental railings and booths, kiosks and slot-machines, and by building tea-parlours, bandstands and pierrot fit-ups out over the shingle. There was also the pier, the centre of life in summer. Here, where the coast started to turn its eastern corner, bathing was dangerous. Coldmouth's holiday posters always pictured the swimming-pool; yet each year, to local disgust, some visitor would risk the sea and drown himself.

Worse than the sea to Coldmouth hotelkeepers was the east wind that, even in summer, raged like a bear about the city. The municipality could offer no alternative to that. It was raging now. One or two elderly residents could be seen huddled within shelters, but no one was out walking that evening. The front was already shuttered and barred against the winter storms.

While Hugo was abroad, he had always imagined the esplanade crowded and tumultuous with the splendours of summer—queues for the tea-shops, queues for ice-cream, queues for box-offices, turnstiles, pier and swimming-pool, and for the kiosks marked 'Ladies' and 'Men'; the white, bank-holiday sun raying out from steel and glass; and stream of feet endlessly shuffling through litter. The air grew heavy with exhaust fumes. Late at night, when the excursion trains and coaches had gone, the promenade would be covered with torn newspaper, orange-peel, banana-skins and ice-cream cups.

Yet most of Hugo's memories of his youth here had a winter background. In summer he had seemed to be lost in a crowd of visitors: it was only when they deserted the place that the people who lived in Coldmouth had a chance to experience life.

The bus moved slowly, quivering in the wind, almost seeming impeded by it, but the end of the promenade came at last. Here, among a few hotels built in the '30s, the houses were small and pleasant. This was Ridley, once a fishing village isolated in the lee of the cliff. Hugo could remember when Ridley was a long tram-ride away and there was half a mile of downland between its first cottages and the last of Coldmouth. Ridley was still regarded by visitors as 'superior' to Coldmouth and some of the hotels advertised themselves as 'exclusive', which meant, so Coldmouth people said, they excluded anyone who could not afford their prices.

Under the flank of the cliff the promenade ended in an oval of tarmac where the bus swung round and stopped. The sudden cutting off of the wind's roar produced an illusion of deafness. Hugo was the only passenger left. When ne stepped down to the tarmac and heard in the silence the sound of his own footsteps, he was conscious of having come to the end of a journey. After eight days' travel on sea and land, he had arrived.

A man was standing on the grass verge under the cliff. Perhaps a passenger for the returning bus—but he made no move toward it. He stood as though he had nothing to do but stand, a delicate, rather elegant figure, some age between fifty and sixty, the wreck of a very handsome man.

As Hugo crossed the road, the man stepped forward and said: "You must be Hugo Fletcher? I am Charles Martyn. I was afraid you might not find your way from here." There came out from him such a warmth of friendliness that Hugo, caught unawares, moved forward eagerly, responding with trust and pleasure, but suddenly, as their hands met, something went wrong. The headmaster's smile failed; he glanced away, seeming to retreat within himself as though his first warmth had been all a mistake. Hugo's reaction was immediate. He may not be all the headmaster had hoped for, but he should be given more chance than this.

Martyn turned and led the way. There was a long silence before he said: "I'm sorry I could not send a car. We have a station-wagon but it got smashed up. It's in a garage at Crowhaven."

Hugo did his best to respond without showing his annoyance at Martyn's attitude to him: "No one hurt, I hope?"

"No," Martyn lingered on the word, then repeated vaguely "No," as though uncertain whether it was the right answer or not. He glanced behind and, without actually looking at Hugo, threw in his direction a brief, uncomfortable smile. When he turned again, he sighed as though harassed to desperation.

7

They were walking along a weedy gravel track that had once been a private drive to Ridley House. When, as a boy, Hugo had come here on bank-holiday trips, the grounds of the house had stretched to the shore. To get up on to the downs, visitors had to take a detour inland. When they reached the cliff-top they could look down on the red-brick house with its many narrow windows that were always covered with cream-coloured blinds. It was the home of a family that seemed never to be at home. In those days Hugo had thought Ridley unimaginably magnificent, but never as exciting and desirable as its neighbour on the cliffs, the Webleys' house.

He was suddenly half-choked by excitement at the thought of the nearness of the Webleys' house. He was returning to Coldmouth but he would be beyond the city's vulgarity, an individual set apart at Ridley: a critic, not to be criticised, who could stroll for a mile across the downs and enter the gates of the Webleys' house and knock at the door that stood within the enormous classical porch—a visitor to be treated with respect! A visitor for young Mrs. Webley!

Why, he might even go this evening.

The excitement of the thought was so nearly painful to him, he tried to distract himself by asking: "Is the house far?" knowing exactly how far it was. His tone, without his intending it, was one of suspended irritation. It startled Martyn, who said: "Not far. No, no, not far," and he glanced round again, this time with a gesture of nervous apology as though conscious his silence might be taken by the newcomer as a slight.

Ridley's gateway now stood three hundred yards back from the road—a dilapidated wooden gate on which was the

sign 'Ridley House Preparatory School'. Across the park—
not much more than a large neglected lawn over which
trees, few and unhindered, stretched themselves like eagles—
tall red chimneys rose above a sombre tangle of ilexes, bays
and monkey-puzzle trees. Martyn, with what seemed an
effort, started to explain that most of the Ridley House
grounds had been bought by the council when Ridley
village became absorbed by the Coldmouth municipality.
Hugo knew all that.

He put down his suitcase, flexed his aching arm and gazed
toward the house. The headmaster, hearing him pause,
looked round enquiringly, then said: "I suppose, after
Egypt, England must seem very fresh and green." Without
waiting for a reply, he hurried on again so that Hugo
imagined he would abandon him if he could.

Because of this, he followed the more slowly. He
remembered that when he had come on excursions in the
past, a small boy with other small boys, he could never risk
being abandoned. He was on edge all the time, always
believing there was a plot afoot to leave him behind. But
now he had life in hand. People did not abandon him; he
abandoned them. He thrust them away, as he had thrust
Tilly into Cyril Webley's arms. He had learnt the trick of
indifference. Now he strolled after Martyn, his every
footstep declaring indifference and, at the same time,
letting it be known he felt some courtesy was due to a man
who had just invested his capital in the place.

Suddenly Martyn turned and, seeing how far he had left
Hugo behind, he hurried back, saying: "I am so sorry. I
was forgetting you had that bag. Let me take a turn."

The bag contained little more than Hugo's needs for a

9

night or two. He flushed and held to it. "No," he said, "it's not heavy. I can manage it. There's not much in it. My cases are being sent from the ship."

Martyn, walking on again, went with self-conscious slowness, glancing back every few minutes, so that Hugo was ashamed of himself, knowing—as he had known all the time, of course—that the headmaster had hurried not to escape Hugo but to escape—what? The wolves of anxiety?

Hugo reflected that had he inherited, with his mother's looks, her ease in company, he might have won Martyn in a moment. At that mention of Egypt and England, he would have talked as readily as she used to talk. Instead of inflicting this silence that drove his companion inwards, he would, without any embarrassment at all, have made Martyn listen to a description of everything he had seen and felt since his arrival at twilight yesterday. Probably Martyn would have been grateful for the distraction. He would have thought: 'This fellow's going to liven things up at Ridley.' Well, Hugo could not do it. Had he been paralysed, he would not have found speech more difficult: but he began, in his own mind, to re-live his return from the time the ship docked at Liverpool and he had leaned with the other passengers over the rail to stare at England. The greyness of the evening: the brilliant colour of the bib of grass before the Liver building: the forgotten colours of a northern country. Everyone was wildly excited, asking one another which was the more extraordinary—the grass or the double-decker buses that, small and red, circled it like clockwork toys.

When the port authorities released them, the passengers,

who, on the voyage, had formed so intimate a community, began to fall apart. They began to look worried, dislocated, each remembering he had a family and ties that must now displace shipboard friendships as reality displaces mirage. Hugo, who was called to no family, and now could not even feel the impulse that had brought him home, stood alone by the rail dreading the moment of going ashore. He watched the others off the ship and waved to them as they disappeared out of his life. He watched their baggage follow. Everyone else was catching an evening train. He had arranged to spend one more night aboard, then to take the London express that left at six next morning. He would reach London in daylight: he would have time to look around: nothing would come upon him unawares.

Next morning it was raining: a steady drizzle, the first he had seen for years. The dawn was breaking as the train drew out. The grey of the sky turned over against a darker grey. It seemed bogged down by a weight of water. As the light struggled through, he saw distances crowded with rain-fogged trees. Everything was choked with foliage. He remembered particularly, in an area of fine black shale, an enclosure littered with rusty scrap-iron: and even here grass, chickweed, docken and nettle had found root, making more sinister this unfamiliar, wet-shining ugliness. Through the rain-obscured air there loomed, menacingly near at times, gas-works, kilns, iron-foundries, cement coolers, power-stations, goods yards. He felt stifled by them. He had never meant to come back—and yet here he was, unreasonably returned, walking now in a silvery world without brilliance or shadow that he had taken for the natural order of things until he acquired, in Egypt, a taste for space and sunshine.

He realised now that he was walking in the very centre of the path to avoid the verge, yet he knew this grass, for all its dangerous richness, was innocent enough.

He said aloud: "No snakes here."

"What?" Charles Martyn swung round, startled again. "No snakes?" he laughed. "Oh, no. No. Nothing like that here."

They had reached the belt of trees and another gate. On one side there was a large lime still in its summer green. What a soft, upholstered country this was! Beyond the evergreens was a formal garden of dahlias and michaelmas daisies.

For the first time in his life, Hugo was close to Ridley House.

Martyn said: "The original Ridley House, alas! was burnt down in 1880. This horror was put up in its place."

Hugo did not know what comment to make. He was, as his fellow passengers had done when they reached Liverpool, replacing a mirage with a reality, and, for him, the mirage of his memory overhung like a haze the details of the house. He supposed it was—yes, clearly it was, a horror. And the cream blinds were still drawn in most of the rooms (even now, it seemed, something was to remain hidden from him!) and some were torn and most were dirty. The whole house surprised him by its shabby look.

They passed through a porch, shaped like a Gothic church porch, into the vaulted, chilly gloom of a large hall, Here there was a dining-table surrounded by two or three dozen chairs. From the tiled chequer-board of the floor rose a double stairway surmounted by a gallery. Stairs, gallery and the panelling which covered the walls were carved in the manner of a reredos so that the hall, for all its size, seemed congested.

Martyn turned about as though bewildered by his own house. No one appeared. There was no sound of life. He murmured: "I don't know. I don't know." He glanced at Hugo as though he were a problem to be solved, then he said: "My wife's out. I think Mrs. Prosser must be out, too. She does the housekeeping—but I believe I know which is your room."

He led Hugo upstairs to the gallery, where hung a row of portraits so dark that only the pallid oval on each showed them to be portraits.

"Most of the classrooms are there." He nodded to the passage that led from the right of the gallery. "The dormitory is on the top floor. Our sleeping quarters are down here," he turned to the left and opened a door. "I'm sure this room is for you."

Hugo's immediate hope was that Martyn had made a mistake: that when Mrs. Martyn returned she would say that some other, much pleasanter, room was intended for him. This was merely a sliver cut off a large bedroom of the past and it had the unsettling air of a room too tall for its width. Its furniture—a few Edwardian pieces—over-whelmed it.

Martyn said: "I expect you'd like to unpack. When you come down you'll find me pottering in the garden."

When he was alone, Hugo looked from the window. The room was at the back of the house and overlooked a lawn planted here and there with standard rose trees. Beyond, a chalk-pit, filled with trees, was cut like half a bowl into the first rise of the downs. On the Ridley side some houses—

odd little bungalows that he later learnt to call 'pre-fabs'—were climbing up the grass slopes where no other houses had ever been before.

Ridley had always been protected and blinkered by the downs, yet Hugo felt discontented at this narrow view. For some reason he had imagined himself gazing from his window straight into the distance where stood the Webleys' house . . .

He left the window and, throwing himself on the bed, he stared at the ceiling, where the heavy ornamentation had scarcely suggested its motif before it disappeared into the partition wall. The scrap of pattern, impertinent as the flutings on a slice of bridal cake, detonated his sense of having been cheated.

Ridley House had failed him—yet he could blame no one but himself. From his first reading of the advertisement in the *Educational Times*, his first knowing that the old Ridley House of picnic days had been turned into a school, he had been possessed by the need to come here. During his years in Menteh he had saved money systematically—there had been nothing on which to spend it, anyway—with some vague idea of one day returning to England a prosperous man. To England, but not to Coldmouth. Coldmouth was the last place he wanted to see again; yet he had known he must buy the interest in Ridley which Martyn offered. It seemed to him if he failed to do so, his money would be worthless to him. He would cease to have a purpose in life.

When he first answered the advertisement, someone else had started negotiations for the partnership and Hugo had worked himself into a fever of fear that this, the greatest opportunity his life had offered, would be lost to him. But the earlier buyer withdrew and Hugo took his place. The contract was sent him; he signed it and returned it: then reaction chilled him like a plunge into cold water. He became filled with suspicions. Why had the first buyer withdrawn? What was wrong with the place? He had employed to negotiate on his behalf a well-known Coldmouth firm of solicitors called Cowan and Copley. He wrote Mr. Copley a long, querulous letter, all but accusing him of failure to protect his interests. He received in reply bland reassurances. Hugo's spirits crept back to their normal temperature.

During the weeks before his departure he began to see in his mind, like a visionary, places in Coldmouth that he had almost forgotten—places that he now knew no longer existed. In reality the centre of the town was destroyed, Ridley was ugly and comfortless, the downs, even, were being built over. . . .

He jumped up suddenly, impatient to get up to the clifftop and make sure the Webleys' house had not changed with the rest.

There was a basin with running water in his room. He washed and shaved, hearing all the time, from somewhere outside, the to and fro of a lawn-mower. This was a sound he had not heard for so long, he could not at first identify it. When he was ready he glanced from the window and saw Charles Martyn, coatless but elegant still, cutting grass that looked short enough already.

Hugo would, he supposed, be kept by Martyn, to talk or to look round the school. For a moment he felt impatient, then his resolution paused and he was relieved that he need not yet look at the Webleys' house. He would have endless time to contemplate that visit.

The house was empty-sounding and getting dark. He was guided to the lawn by daylight showing through an open back door. Martyn had just turned and was marching back along the length of grass, his eyes fixed on the ground, his face set as though he were obsessed by his task. Hugo stood, waiting to be seen. Martyn, when he looked up, seemed surprised as though he had forgotten his visitor, then he took on an air of strained affability: "Ah, there you are!" he said and looked round for his coat.

Hugo, discouraged by the certainty Martyn was being sociable under duress, said at once: "Please don't let me interrupt. I was thinking of going for a walk."

"But you should have tea."

"I had some on the train."

"Oh!" No longer preparing to join Hugo, Martyn relaxed and smiled, and indicated the chalk-pit spinney: "You can get out to the downs through there. So we'll expect you about supper-time? My wife should be back by then."

Hugo set off, waving a hand to Martyn with a movement of extreme carelessness. He told himself if his company were so unwelcome he would remove it without ceremony. When he passed into the masking trees, he listened for the sound of the mower to start up again, but it did not start, and he imagined Martyn, relieved of an unwelcome guest, returning to whatever occupation Hugo's arrival had interrupted. He thought: 'I can manage. In Menteh I managed with precious little.'

In Menteh there had been four of them: Père Legouis of

the Mission, Aston, who had married a Coptic wife and had come south to escape her relatives, and Abdul Fatteh, who owned the sugar factory. While here—here there might be a world of possibilities beyond Ridley. He was no longer poor. He had returned to quite another life. At the thought of it, at the thought of climbing up into view of the house where Tilly now lived, he felt slightly sick with excitement. He paused to recover himself and saw ahead the gate that led from the spinney to the grass-furred, sloping flank of the downland. He looked round for an excuse to pause. There was an iron seat beneath the trees. He sat down and took out his cigarette-case. He would smoke one cigarette before he went out through the gate.

He looked at his watch. It was six o'clock. This was the time at which they used to gather in Abdul's riverside garden—the four of them close in a relationship that comprised little more than curiosity about the details of each other's daily life. What else was there to discuss in a village of a dozen villas, whitewashed boxes as bare inside as out, and the ridiculous block of flats? This little nucleus of Menteh's 'aristocracy' was crowded round with mud houses, the whole forming, in the midst of the bean-fields with their dulcet evening scent, a radiant point of heat, dirt, flies, lice and stench. He had longed to get away from that tiny inquisitive circle. Before he did escape, his exasperation with each of his three friends had become a chronic ache. He did not regret them now, but he felt the mental discomfort of jarred habit. His unfamiliar present made Abdul's garden desirable, so that he remembered only the fragrance of jasmine and of lemon trees, the sweet coffee and the effortlessness of warm, early evening.

17

Absorbed as he was into Menteh's sunset air, he dropped his cigarette-stub to the path and stared, worried by the change in the English light. The damp asphalt, stuck over with yellow, five-fingered leaves, glowed as though incandescent. He looked up. For the first time since his arrival in England, he saw the sun—or, rather, as much of it as one might see of a bonfire in a fog. As the light's colour deepened, it touched with a red gilding the moisture on the tree trunks and fencing.

He looked round slowly, finding himself in a sort of nest of trees, and heard the silence broken by excited birds. The air smelt of wet mould and leaves becoming mould, and of wood smoke that pervaded it so subtly there was no telling mist from smoke.

"How strange it is!" he said aloud, feeling himself shut by trees into a nursery past of Christmas cards and calendars, coloured supplements and *Chatterbox* covers, all glowing so that he seemed to be within a peep-show. A chestnut-burr fell and broke beside him. As he picked it up a chestnut fell into his hand, a marble of polished wood with a rough, mildewed navel.

"Real!" he said. It was all real—the bark of the trees, the patches of silver damp, green damp, fungi, the deeply rich scent, the red-gold where the sun penetrated the branches and touched down on the sheeny ground. Suddenly he was caught back into his childhood anxieties and the claustrophobia of limited power. He was filled with nervous apprehensions as though he were back in the school world he had hated and from which there had been no refuge but his home. He sometimes had nightmares that he was a child again, again trapped among fears of things

18

imperfectly understood. Once that dream had been so vividly oppressive that, waking and finding it only a dream, he had cried with relief.

He jumped up. The past was past. He made for the iron gate that, set in a holly hedge, was rusty, broken and unlatched. The ground rose from it. Where the up-slope was easiest climbers had worn off the surface grass, making a chalk path noduled with flints. The grass was coarse and grey and had, in the increasing sunlight, the glint of steel.

When Hugo reached the cliff-top he came to a standstill and gazed toward the Webleys' house. It was there all right. Its white, windowless flank rose above trees that had, he noticed, grown wilder, thicker and darker in his absence. It was a solitary house and stood exposed on its headland looking at nothing but the sea.

Something, small and beetle-black, moving on the Crowhaven road, shifted his gaze to the left. Only a car—but it might have come from the house. Tilly might be inside it. The last time he had seen her, after she had told him she was finished with him, she had jumped into Cyril Webley's car. She and Webley had been married a few days later. The car recalled that rebuff so acutely, he felt panic at the thought she might pass near him. He turned his back on the house and, skirting the chalk-pit, he hurried down among the bungalows and took the road to the promenade. The car was catching up on him—then he heard it turn into Ridley High Street. Swinging round, he was in time to catch a glimpse of the driver. A man: and alone.

Disappointed, he let his pace flag and he began to doubt whether he could, after all, impress Tilly. He was still only a school-teacher. As for Ridley House—at close quarters it was decayed and ugly, and appeared now to be of no importance at all. But the Webleys' house, standing there like a bastion on the cliff, that was a house indeed! It had been built about a hundred years before by an actor who was still famous in Coldmouth as an actor because he had built this house in this remote, romantic spot. Parents passing on the train to and from Crowhaven would point it out to their children and say: "That was Sir Jason Sparkes' house," and when asked: "Who was Sir Jason Sparkes?" would answer: "He was a famous actor," so that Coldmouth children, when they went to live elsewhere, would be surprised to find no one had heard of him. His son had lived and died in the house, becoming there a very old bachelor who sometimes drove in a dog-cart into Coldmouth, dressed, even in the '30s, like the illustrations to *Sherlock Holmes*.

In this way the house had survived the period of Gothic taste. Severely square with an ornamented cornice and a classical portico, it aroused curiosity but not admiration in Coldmouth, being described as 'a great barn of a place' and 'too plain for my liking', so there had been some surprise when old Webley, the draper, who could afford to build himself anything he liked, chose to buy the house on the death of Irving Sparkes. Webley not only 'paid through the nose for it' but spent 'thousands' putting in central heating and a vast window to frame the sea, and levelling the garden so that the basement could be converted into a dining-room with french windows opening to a lawn. Hugo had seen these wonders with his own eyes—once, and briefly—when he and two other boys had been taken by Cyril on a half-holiday to play ping-pong on the dining-room table. Hugo had been invited because he was, quite accidentally, within earshot when the others were invited. Who but Cyril Webley would have felt impelled for that reason to include him? No one at St. Aubyn's had considered Hugo's feelings, for whose feelings had he considered?

Anyway, he had been one of those who had seen inside the house: but, like Cyril himself, he had not boasted of it. He was not so easily impressed. The boasting had been done by those on the fringe of the Webley set who wished it known that they had seen the dining-room with its staircase curving up round the wall, and looked out at the sea from the vast sitting-room window, and trodden the carpets that had a spongy rubber beneath them, and experienced the central heating. One boy had even been in the house when the Webleys gave a dinner-party, and he and Cyril had hung over the banister to watch the guests in evening dress—famous people, some of them town councillors, and all owners of large shops or hotels—descend to dine.

'And now,' thought Hugo, his spirits roused again, 'I am your nearest neighbour,' and he saw within his mind Tilly crossing the pneumatic carpet toward him, she scarcely able, in her surprise, to speak his name:

"Hugo!"

How he would behave he was still uncertain. All he had thought and felt about her during his years abroad was fogged over now by his anticipation of coming face to face with her as, surely, he one day must.

Even now, turning the corner on to the promenade, he might . . . but there was no one there. Not even a complete stranger. The wind rushed at him along the deserted front. He leant a while over the rail and saw the sun touch the horizon beyond a sea that was grey-blue like a harebell.

In the distance the brickwork of the dockyard area was spot-lit by the rich terra-cotta of the sunset. When this was suddenly cut off, the whole place took on the bleak air of near winter. He remembered how he had hated this season in the past. He liked it no better now.

He longed—yes, he wildly longed—to be back in Egypt: not because Egypt had meant so much to him but because there his money had been intact. There he could imagine the future as he wished. Its possibilities were endless. Now he had spent his money and he knew what he had bought. The future was this same old promenade where he had walked away so many wretched evenings in the past.

As he went on, he considered asking Martyn to release him from his contract: "Please return me my money and let me go." Well, there was little hope of that. But would he, perhaps, return two-thirds of the money? As he remembered the sea of legal documents that flowed between him and his old freedom, Hugo doubted whether even two-thirds could be got back. Let the buyer beware. And the buyer, huddling his shoulders from the English cold, tried to put his folly from his head.

Half-way along the promenade, he crossed the road to look at a tobacconist's shop over which was written: 'Cleaver, late Lawson'. So Lawson had retired? or died? Well, that made one enemy the less! As he neared the pier he could see the meagre population of winter circulating round the entrance. A concert was advertised. Young men waited for their girls.

A few strollers had been brought out by the late sunlight. Unconsciously Hugo straightened his shoulders, tilted back his head and looked about him with a languid and insolent indifference. But no one responded. Many of the passers-by did not even return his stare; the others glanced back with so genuine an unconcern, he might have been in a city of strangers. Only one face was familiar and that seemed not so much a face he had known as a badly drawn copy of it. Even that face passed him with an unchanging expression.

He began to realise he was forgotten. He had gone away notorious and condemned; he had returned to indifference. Battle would not be joined after all. He felt relieved, yet disappointed. He also felt tired. He had not, as he pretended to Martyn, had tea on the train. He had eaten nothing since breakfast.

Opposite the pier was the Gala Café. He stood on the pavement and looked across at the word 'Gala' written in red neon. It was a large café above a row of shops. The stairs that led up to it used to be of flecked composition stone, rather orange in colour. He crossed over and saw they were unchanged. For no reason at all, the sight of them made him apprehensive. No reason at all. Indeed, he could, if he wished, afford to go where he had never before thought of going—the Royal Beach Hotel or the Bristol: but those places meant nothing to him. What he wanted was to enter the 'Gala' again and buy himself a slap-up tea.

"Well, here goes!" he said and ascended the stairs, prepared for anything but his own shock at the dinginess of the place. He paused at the top of the stairs, deflated, his appetite gone, and would have bolted had not a waitress seen him and motioned him to her table. He sat down.

Before the war this had been for him the desired centre of

the world. For all the young people here it had been the centre of Coldmouth. They would come early to get a seat near the dance floor. Hugo and Tilly had had to be content with a less conspicuous seat so that the waitress would not resent so much their sitting all evening over their single cups of coffee. It was here he had watched Tilly go on to the dance floor with Webley. Knowing she was finished with him, he had believed his life was ended.

Now he gave the waitress a smile of condescending good-fellowship and ordered tea, buttered toast, hot scones, jam and cakes. The girl stared at him coldly. They did not 'do' toast these days and never had scones. She might, if she tried, find a cake or two left on the other tables.

His look was so crestfallen that she troubled to explain that the Gala's 'Elegant Teas' were off at five-thirty and it was now twenty past six. The 'snacks' came on at six-thirty, but she might, as a favour, be able to let him have one now. Her attitude dwindled Hugo's money in his pockets. He thanked her as fervently as he was expected to do and asked for beans on toast.

Aston, who had had a visit home in 1948, had said: "Everything there is either difficult or impossible." Well, one would get used to it.

While Hugo waited he looked about him. He could have sworn that before the war the place was larger and lighter, and the dance floor twice the size. He recognised the brown wall-paper smudged with gold, the galleons on the age-yellowed lamp-shades, and the central light screened with oblongs of yellow and orange glass. It was all the same, but worn and dusty. It had become a sad place, while he was sad no longer.

24

By the time he had eaten his beans on toast, the tables had been set for evening 'snacks'. He was near the door and watched people coming in: young people meeting here after shops and offices closed. They looked to him a colourless lot.

It was not only the café that had shrunk and grown dim during his years abroad. Its patrons, once the famous figures of Coldmouth, had become nonentities. Before the war he had been an elementary school-teacher and Tilly had worked in a shop, yet they had been individuals, distinguishable from the rest. The girls that came here then had been exciting; the men enviable. Surely there had been a glitter over them all!

He would never come to the Gala Café again.

*   *   *   *

When Hugo got back to Ridley House he found the front door ajar. A dim light came from a wooden chandelier high above the hall. Martyn, who must have been listening for him, put his head out of a room at the end and said: "This is the sitting-room. We have meals in here during the holidays."

As Hugo went upstairs he looked at the row of portraits and saw stare back at him, from three of the five painted faces, Charles Martyn's mild, blue eyes.

Hugo, who half-unconsciously had discounted the portraits as 'props'—the sort of thing that might be picked up second-hand and hung somewhere, at a safe distance, to impress parents—was ruffled by the realisation that these were genuine family portraits. The fact seemed to place him at a disadvantage. After a moment he shook it off by telling himself that Martyn, family or no family, had needed his money. There was also the wife! Martyn, in one of his letters, said she had been an actress. An actress meant to Hugo the sort of little blonde girl who played in the summer shows on the pier. He had seen a serious play only once in his life, on his one visit to London, and that had left on him an impression of a world so remote and mystifying he could not associate it with anyone who might touch upon his own life. Indeed, he had almost forgotten all about it.

Well, this Mrs. Martyn, the ex-actress, was not likely to over-awe Hugo. She might even be rather fun. There was also Brian Martyn, the son of a previous marriage, described by his father as 'our administrator'. Hugo began to feel impatient to get down to supper, but when he entered the sitting-room only Martyn was there.

Seeing Hugo glance round at the empty chairs—large chairs covered with worn and faded chintz—Martyn said: "I am afraid my wife is not back yet." He added as though in explanation of her absence: "She has a brother in Coldmouth."

"Are they a Coldmouth family?"

"No. Her brother was sent here during the war . . ." Martyn broke off as though in mid-sentence and a silence came down between them. He was standing by the fireplace with one foot on the fender. The fire had just been lit, probably by Martyn himself, and a tail of smoke quivered up coldly from three damp logs. The room was pleasant enough with its chintz and mahogany. Hugo, left in the air with nothing to say, looked over his shoulder at the books lining two walls. Their number and bindings made him feel at a loss. He could only hope that Martyn, for want of anything else, would not begin asking him: "Have you read this?" and "Have you read that?" for he was aware he had read nothing that would seem worth reading to a man with a library like this.

Martyn said: "Mrs. Prosser should be back by now. I have no idea where she has gone."

"Mrs. Prosser is the matron, I suppose?"

"No, she's a sort of housekeeper. She used to be my wife's dresser."

"I suppose it isn't easy to get help these days?"

"Not easy. Not easy," murmured Martyn, glancing about him as though at a loss to know what to do with Hugo, then he smiled suddenly, his whole expression growing vivid and eager, and said: "Will you take a glass of sherry?" He went to a corner cupboard and, standing with his back to the room, head bent, he fumbled for several moments with a ring of keys before finding the right one and getting the bottle out.

Hugo, on edge, would have begged him not to trouble but knew the not troubling would be, if anything, more painful to both of them. In order that he need not suffer with Martyn's fumblings, he turned and examined the objects on the mantelshelf: a carriage clock, two china figures with broken fingers, a little box (a snuff-box, he supposed) made of some green stone ornamented with silver on which a crest was engraved. He fixed his eyes on the crest, envious of all it signified, irritated by his own sense of deprivation, yet elated by the thought he would invite Tilly to tea here—here, in this room with the leather-bound books and the crested snuff-box—and introduce her to the Martyns with an easy indifference, a contempt that would discount the lot of them!

27

"Now," said Martyn as he put bottle and glasses on the table, "this will warm us up," but the sherry, very dry and pale as winter sunlight, no more dispelled the chill than did the smoke from the logs. Holding their glasses, they stood over the fire, not in hope of warmth, but feeling that the smoke's movement and their contemplation of it gave them excuse for silence. At last Hugo thought of something to say:

"I look forward to meeting your son."

Martyn put out his foot in its fine, black, narrow-toed shoe and touched one of the logs. A flame appeared. He made no other response to Hugo, who began to feel irritated. Was he to be made to feel his every remark was an indiscretion? Well, he would say nothing more. Let Martyn deal with the situation. This decision seemed to convey itself to the headmaster, who, making an effort, said: "Tell me about your job in Upper Egypt. It must have been interesting to keep you there so long."

Long? Six years. It was true that six years of Menteh would seem an eternity to most people, yet when he looked back on his life there, Hugo saw it with its repeating pattern of days superimposed each on the other so that together they held no more substance than a dream. As for teaching! Well, he might have said all by saying he had made no effort to combat the limitations of his pupils—but that was not the sort of bright remark his new headmaster would expect from him.

"Yes," he said, pausing and giving the matter some unaccustomed thought before he described how the boys were quick and clever when young, but too ready to imagine they knew everything as soon as they knew something; how they grew steadily duller and more slothful as they grew older until for most of them any effort, save that which satisfied their three needs, money, food and sex, was a waste of time. But one had to remember that much of this dullness resulted from under-feeding and the Nile valley's endemic disease, bilharzia. Malaria did not help, either.

As Hugo expounded the social problems of Egypt, he began to feel a glow of self-congratulation that he had, almost without knowing it, picked up so much information on these subjects. Owing nothing now to the Egyptian regime, he was free to express indignation against the pashas who chose not to deal with a disease that could have been easily wiped out. Their policy was to keep the fellah safely unthinking in the lethargy of ill-health. He realised that now, no longer oppressed himself by monotony and the inescapable heat, he really was indignant; and, as his indignation was reflected in Martyn's face, they felt, in their mutual right-thinking, joined in a warmth of sympathy.

"You liked the people?"

"Yes," Hugo replied, truthfully enough. In Egypt, where Europeans are easily irritated, he had been maddened by the fecklessness, dishonesty and dirt of the Egyptians, so that at times he had hated the lot of them. Now, remembering their good-humour, he said: "One wanted to help them."

Martyn nodded approval. He was about to speak, but hearing the front door slam he said only: "My wife. Excuse me."

As he went out, Hugo had a glimpse of the woman in the hall—a woman of medium height, of extreme and challenging beauty—then the door slid between them. It did not close; it was held by some anti-slamming device so that Hugo could clearly hear Martyn's voice, urgent and anxious, saying:

"My dear, Mr. Fletcher has arrived."

"Has he?" Mrs. Martyn's voice was deep and had a tone of tipsy ridicule.

"Won't you come in and meet him?"

"No, I'm tired."

"But you'll be down for supper?"

"I'm not hungry. I'm going to bed."

"Where is Mrs. Prosser?"

"It's her evening out."

"So it is. But, Kyra . . ."

"Oh, do shut up. You can deal with him alone, can't you? It's none of my business."

Hugo could hear her heels tapping as she went upstairs. He felt slighted and made no reply when Martyn looked in to say: "Supper won't be long. Have some more sherry."

After the door had shut again, Hugo looked at the snuff-box and thought: 'Probably bought it second-hand.' He remembered that at St. Aubyn's once the rugger team had taken to wearing crest-engraved signet rings bought from a pawnbroker near the harbour. Hugo, too poor to follow this fashion, had been delighted to notice that the boy who sat next to him had sported a leopard one day and a swan the next. Hugo had made the most of what he then thought a riotous joke, and he had never forgotten it. Now he crossed to the bookcases and took one of the calf-bound books from the shelves. A coat of arms was gilt-tooled on the front. He compared the crest with that on the box. It was the same.

"Genuine set-up," he whispered to himself.

Disconcerted, he hurried the book back to its place and was by the fire again when Martyn entered with a tray.

"Here we are," said Martyn, putting on the table knives, forks, bread and two plates of fried sausages and tomatoes. " 'Pot-luck', I'm afraid. My wife has come in tired. You must excuse her. Can you eat this sort of food? It's very rough."

Hugo scarcely noticed what he was eating, filled as he was with an acute sense of disadvantage. He wanted somehow to let Martyn know that his own family had known its better days. His early poverty had resulted only from his father's folly. But what did Martyn know of Hugo's early poverty? In any case, he was not going to give himself away with protestations of that sort. He had bought his position here. Let him and Martyn stand equal on a solid basis of cash.

He said: "Your wife was on the stage, wasn't she?"

Martyn agreed she had been.

"I got a glimpse of her just now. Her face was familiar. I suppose there used to be a lot of pictures of her about."

"Maybe. I'm afraid I do not know. I have had little to do with the theatre myself."

The sense of strain had returned. Martyn asked no more questions about Egypt. Both men relaxed a little when they heard Kyra Martyn's steps returning down the stairs.

She came in rubbing her hands together and gave no explanation of herself. Hugo, standing up to be introduced, was disappointed. The impression of her beauty had been a trick of distance. She was a woman grown haggard and over-thin in middle age. There were marks like bruises under her eyes. She gave Hugo a shrewd, assessing stare which, when met by his awareness, she hid with the sudden

31

flash of a smile. Shuddering elaborately, she spread her thin
fingers to the fire and said: "Cold. Cold. The long violins
at it again."

She was as uneasy as her husband seemed to be. Hugo
wondered what was the matter with the pair of them.

Martyn went out to make some coffee and Hugo, left
alone with Kyra, said: "I was just telling Mr. Martyn, when
I saw you just now, your face seemed rather familiar. I must
have seen photographs of you somewhere. Or perhaps you
were in films?"

She gave a short, bleak laugh and said: "I suppose you
saw *Message*."

"Was that a film?"

"No," she sounded impatient, "a play. A play that had a
long run in London. *Message from the Outside World*. Hell of
a name for a play."

He recalled suddenly that that was the play he had seen on
his one night in London: "Of course," he agreed, "*Message
from the Outside World*."

On his way up in the train that morning, twelve years
before, he had heard two young naval officers talking, not of
the play, but of the actress who took the chief part. One had
compared her with some great foreign actresses; the other
had said she was the most beautiful creature he had ever
seen. Hugo, who had thought of going to a successful
musical show, was suddenly determined to see this woman.
The theatre was crowded. Hugo stood at the back of the
pit with all the others who had failed to find a seat. The
excitement of the audience had led him to expect something
beyond his imagining, but he was merely bewildered by
what he saw. The woman—this woman here in the room

with him now—had stood between the two panes of a double window, high in the centre of the stage, and gazed out beyond the audience and the immediate consciousness, her face green-white like a water-lily, her eyes and mouth painted so that they seemed more tragic than life. Her darker voice, deep and affecting, was transmitted by some arrangement of microphones, so it had not been muffled by the glass. It touched the nerves, claiming him in spite of himself. Now her voice was hoarse and not pitched to excite an audience. What surprised him most was the fact her eyes were not large or even dark—their colour was a light hazel—and her lips were thin. Her hair, that on the stage had been a brilliant gold catching the light like metal, was now a lightish, greying brown. Had she, he wondered, ever been much of an actress? or was it merely that that illusion of beauty had, together with her symbolical captivity, so possessed the imagination that criticism was stilled? He had left the theatre dazed, uncertain if what he had seen had had meaning or not.

On an impulse, looking at her thin cheeks, he said: "I thought you were wonderful."

She jerked up her head and made an odd, painful noise in her throat, then said exultantly: "What a remarkable play! Remarkable, wasn't it?" insisting on the quality of the play almost as though she could not bear a mention of herself.

"Yes, remarkable!" he felt bound to agree with her.

"Someone said that that solitary figure, that girl, up in the double window, that confined space, expressed all the despair of man's mortality." She glanced round as she spoke and, seeing the sherry bottle, went to it and splashed herself out a glass.

"Such an original play!" she continued after a while. "So full of feeling. A *deep* play, wasn't it? and what a part! To tell you the truth, I have never found another part like it. Really, it was like getting somewhere before you'd started. I had nowhere else to go." She paused, then said flatly: "I came to a full stop. I got married."

"How can you stand it here in Coldmouth?" Hugo asked. "This place is so . . . so hideous."

"But so amusing, don't you think? All that Gothic and Moorish and what-not along the front; and that debased Empire and heaven knows what. Really, it's rather delicious."

Hugo had no idea what she meant by 'amusing' and 'delicious'. He made no reply, feeling, as he did, that a stand he had believed safe had given way under his feet.

"But you prefer London?" she smiled at him.

He was not going to say he had spent only one night there. Feeling too insecure to speak again, he was glad to see Martyn return with the coffee. The headmaster seemed less distracted now but more nervous than before. When he spoke to his wife, he did so in an anxious, humouring way.

"You will have some coffee with us, won't you, Kyra, my dear?"

She did not glance at him or speak to him, but took the cup he offered and, as she sat down, she said to Hugo: "Of course I prefer London, too. I belong there. In a place like this I simply waste my time."

"I hate this place!" Hugo spoke forcefully, scarcely thinking what he was saying.

She looked up, surprised, and said: "Then you won't be sorry you are not staying."

34

Hugo was about to ask what she meant when Martyn broke in: "My dear, I have not told Mr. Fletcher anything."

"Oh!" For the first time since entering, she stared directly at her husband, her glance cold, her chin lifted in dramatic accusation.

Martyn did not meet her eyes but said: "I will tell him in good time. He has only just arrived." His whole air was of a dejected guilt.

Hugo, watching the two of them, apprehended disaster, but the sense of this lifted suddenly as he saw the possibility of escape. His hope was such he could scarcely speak, but he managed to say: "Has it anything to do with the school?"

Martyn drew his breath in through his lips as though preparing to speak, but he said nothing. After several moments' silence, Hugo could not control his impatience. He said: "Is there some question of the school's not opening again?"

Kyra turned aside and lit a cigarette as though she were outside the conversation, Martyn cleared his throat, but it was not until the silence had stretched itself to breaking point that he said: "No, we are not opening next term."

"Perhaps you will explain?"

"I will explain, of course." Martyn straightened his shoulders as though attempting to retain the calm of a man used to authority, but little came of it: "If you'll excuse me now. . . . You've only just arrived. I was not expecting. . . . I had hoped to write you when I received your London address."

"But what has happened? You were all right financially."

"The educational authorities have withdrawn their grant. We can't go on without it."

35

"Surely that implies some serious trouble?"

"Yes." After a pause Martyn said quietly: "May we leave it all until the morning?" His voice faded out on the word. Hugo, who had been irritated that he could get no certainty, was forced to let the matter drop. He looked at Kyra, hoping she might be more willing to explain, but she rose to her feet as he turned towards her. Her cigarette, drooping from her mouth, stuck dryly to her dry lips, and she cocked her head to one side and narrowed her eyes against the smoke.

"I suppose you'll be staying a bit, Mr. Fletcher?"

"Yes," Martyn answered for him, speaking more willingly now. "You must stay a bit, Fletcher. Have a holiday, anyway."

"If you stay," said Kyra, "there's the question of your ration book."

"Oh, my dear," Martyn interrupted gently, "don't worry Mr. Fletcher about that now."

"Very well," she turned away. "Good-night."

As soon as she had left them, Martyn said: "Would you like some more coffee?"

Hugo shook his head, scarcely realising what he had been asked. He was beginning to feel an ecstatic lightness of spirit at the thought of getting his money back. There would be almost nothing he could not do. It was as though some error of the past had, by a miracle, been wiped out. His future was restored to him. In this mood, observing Martyn's desolation, he was filled with compassion for the man. The school must have meant a great deal to him. Hugo said: "I am sorry we are not going to work together."

"I am sorry, too." The headmaster did not look up.

Speech between them was clearly at a standstill and the sense of the delayed explanation was more troubling than silence. Hugo knew Martyn was waiting for him to go. He said: "If you'll excuse me, I'll say 'Good-night'. I want to write some letters."

Martyn rose at once and said: "You must forgive me. I'm still somewhat dazed. It all happened so recently. To tell you the truth, the letter from the Ministry arrived only this morning. Before that I thought we might weather it somehow . . . at least, I told myself we might." He sighed and looked sadly at his visitor, who, lacking any significant information, could make no comment.

When Hugo reached the landing, he smiled at the portraits and said: "I'm sorry. I might have liked you," but he forgot them in a moment. He was sorry for the headmaster, but he did not think there was anything he could do. His life had brushed that of the Martyns and now must move on.

CHAPTER II

HUGO, from habit, was up next morning at six o'clock. Already he had planned his short stay here. He would not walk over to the Webleys' house: instead he would hire a car and drive over. His money, which he saw returning like a gift, made him feel extravagant.

"Hello, Tilly! Just called to see how you are getting on."

"Why, Hugo! When did you arrive in Coldmouth?"

"Couple of days ago."

"Are you here for good?"

"Oh, Lord, no. Off to London tomorrow."

"So soon?"

Yes, so soon. Now he no longer felt afraid of London. He felt afraid of nothing.

He left his room in his dressing-gown, a towel over his arm, but he did not go to the bathroom at the end of the passage. He crossed the landing to the other rooms, the classrooms, determined before he left to see one of those at the front on which the cream-coloured blinds were drawn.

The house was as silent as an empty house. The wood of the panelling and stairs was honey-coloured in the early sunlight. He noticed that the ceiling was also of wood, carved over with conventional roses, from the centre of each of which a point dropped like a stalactite toward the ground.

The effect produced by all this ornamentation was of a miniature mock-Gothic cathedral done on the cheap. At this thought Hugo nearly laughed aloud, for somehow it put Ridley and Coldmouth, the Martyns, the portraits, the green and silver box, all into a category of absurdity that did for the lot of them.

The first doorway across the landing was marked 'Classroom A'. This would do as well as another. He opened it quietly, expecting a sort of half-darkness, but the light diffused through the pale, opaque blinds lit the room more clearly than direct sunlight would have done. A dozen desks, standing in rows of four, had an air of pausing in some private activity. Above the fireplace was a map, pink and yellow on a cerulean sea, the leg-of-mutton shape of South America.

A little platform had been built for the teacher's desk. Behind it was fixed to the wall a large blackboard, on which someone had scribbled two male figures. Hugo's glance passed over them, then, startled, returned. Unable to believe what he had seen, he stepped up to the dais to see the drawing more closely. He stared at it for several moments before jumping down and hurrying from the room. He felt as though he were making a get-away, as though it were he that had cause to feel guilty.

When he had bathed and dressed, he waited in his room for some sound of life in the house. He had two or three green 'Penguins' with him but could not read. In his impatience to get the day started, the present cleared away and the future begun, he seemed to be holding his breath. He lay on his bed, stared at the ceiling and listened. At last someone went downstairs: a woman. That would be the housekeeper, Mrs. Prosser. Later, another woman. He waited, still listening for Martyn's heavier footsteps, but there was only a long silence, during which his impatience became unbearable. He swung off the bed and went down to the sitting-room. The two women were at breakfast. Kyra Martyn was smoking. With one eye shut against the smoke, she glanced at him as though he were not over-welcome, and gave him a casual "Hello."

The table, he saw, was set for only three. His first thought was that he was not expected for breakfast; his second that Martyn had bolted. There would be no explanation, perhaps no money, and there was Mrs. Martyn dissociating herself from the whole thing and eyeing him to see how he was taking it. He said accusingly: "Where is Mr. Martyn?"

"He had a bad night. I left him sleeping."

Her casualness irritated Hugo, so he spoke more sharply than he had intended: "I thought we were going to have a talk this morning."

"Oh!" She gave her head an impatient jerk. "Leave it till the afternoon." She motioned him to the vacant chair, then pushed the toast-rack and coffee-pot towards him. He sat down, reassured, yet made to feel importunate. Still, he cared nothing for Mrs. Martyn's opinion of him. She would have little part in his life.

"You haven't met Mrs. Prosser?" she asked.

Hugo, repelled by Mrs. Prosser's appearance, acknowledged her presence without enthusiasm. Her hair was carroty; her skin veined and dark. She had hard, blue, little eyes, a bulbous nose and a spade-shaped chin. Her extraordinary ugliness affected him like an affront. He was thankful he would not be required to consort with her.

Mrs. Prosser met his nod with a grin that had an almost imbecile width: "Pleased to meet you, I'm sure," she said. He looked away quickly, but in a moment felt drawn to glance back at her. Her face still wore the grin, but she had turned it now towards Kyra, and it had taken on a quality of derision he could only feel was directed against himself. Heavens, what a revolting woman!

Kyra leant back in her chair and with her cigarette moving as she talked, said: "Well, Prossy, we'll have to get something extra for luncheon. You won't forget your Food Book, will you, Mr. Fletcher? You have only to take your passport to the Food Office. It's a pre-fab building near the remains of the City Hall."

As soon as he had eaten breakfast, he left the house with his passport in his pocket, but he went out through the spinney and climbed first to the downs. The matter of his visit to Tilly being now settled in his mind, he scarcely glanced at the Webleys' house, but crossed the grass to the road that skirted the railway line. This was the line along which the London trains, after they had called at Cold-mouth, followed the coast to Crowhaven. The children who picnicked here would watch for them—the boat trains, the trains full of people from London who were on their way to foreign countries: unique trains, the most important sights of the day. He got through the wire and climbed up the railway bank. At the top he stood for a long time over-looking the country beyond. The downs in the distance were as they had always been; their whale curves interlaced, spotted with dark trees and here and there slashed with chalk. But the near, the once familiar, country had been ploughed and planted, and was now cut into stubbled fields that looked neglected. He turned away angrily. Anyone might have known that ground was not worth cultivating; but in war-time—a time, it seemed, when freedom and beauty were considered scarcely decent—even the land must suffer. Before the war there had been large flocks here of blunt-faced, close-woolled sheep, but now no sheep: only the dismal cultivation stretching out like a continuation of the dismal town. That Coldmouth had lost even its common land—the near downland that had always been the goal of special holidays—seemed to complete his severance from home.

He made his way down to the esplanade and set out for the Food Office.

When he thought again how narrow had been his second escape from this place, he felt something near panic. Had Martyn advertised and he seen the advertisement a year, even six months, before, his money would have been sunk in the school and perhaps lost with it. What would have become of him without his money, the sign and substance of his liberty?

"God!" he murmured, and for a moment he was shaken as though he had skirted a cliff-edge. The shock left him with a sense of urgency about the money question. He must get it settled.

When he left the Food Office with his new ration book it was barely midday. He walked slowly back through the bombed area to Ridley High Street, a long street of shops that ran parallel with the promenade. As he neared the Ridley Arms, he saw pressed against the engraved glass of the saloon door the white shirt of a man drawing the bolts. The shirt disappeared. He entered a bar that was empty and smelling sourly of beer and stale tobacco.

Within five minutes half a dozen other customers had drifted in and stood in a semi-circle, each with drink in hand, silently gazing at the door. At last one of them, in the tone of someone manfully facing a fact, announced loudly: "Nip in the air these days."

"Must expect it," said another, and silence returned.

The barman, who spoke in a bright, shrill, eunuch's voice, looked at Hugh standing alone and said: "Having a late holiday, like?"

"Yes and no," Hugo replied, lapsing into the local language.

"I see." The barman nodded as though he understood perfectly.

Hugo moved a little nearer and, making a slight gesture to incite confidence, asked quietly: "Any more news about that school up the road?"

The barman, round, cheerful, given to tricks of behaviour, raised an eyebrow: "Oh, what school would that be?" he asked. "I'm new here."

"Ridley School," said Hugo.

The semi-circle of local men seemed struck to stillness. Each man stood rooted, head bowed, in the attitude of one who knew but a thousand pounds would not get a word from him. Suddenly the first speaker drained his glass and put it on the counter. "Well, so long," he said, and the others answered: "So long." He left with decision.

During this departure the barman leant over the counter and stared purposefully at the group. As soon as it was static again, he said: "You heard anything about a school, Harry?"

The man appealed to looked round sideways and gave

43

Hugo a quick glance, then he stared at the floor again and smiled into himself. "There've been stories going round," he said.

"It's been closed down, hasn't it?" Hugo appealed to him.

"Something like that." The man raised his eyebrows and looked at his companions with a conspiratorial smirk.

Hugo knew these people. His old irritation welled up in him and with it his old desire to do and say something outrageous, to hit out at their self-satisfaction, their constant certainty that they were the clever ones, the ones that knew everything, the ones who were always right. He kept patience and asked: "Wasn't there something in the papers?"

For some moments no one spoke, then an old man, probably a survivor of the village that had been inundated by Coldmouth, said gently: "Not much in the papers. They didn't catch no one, you see."

With a deliberation of manner meant to convey his opinion of the others, Hugo invited the old man and the barman to drink with him. As the old man joined him at the bar counter, he felt the others pricked to attend to their conversation and he defeated them by discussing nothing but the weather.

On his way back to the school, his anxiety and suspicion rose so that he could scarcely control his impulse to break into a run. Martyn, surely, was a man who would keep his word! But Hugo trusted no one. He could imagine even that that crew in the public-house had been part of a conspiracy to tell him nothing. When he entered the school he strode angrily across the hall to the sitting-room, then

44

paused, growing calm as he heard through the open french windows the sound of the lawn-mower.

Martyn was out in the garden again; again cutting grass that did not need cutting. Hugo sensed in him an anxiety like his own. Well, they might get it all over before luncheon.

The headmaster looked round as Hugo called "Goodmorning." He left the mower and came inside at once.

"I am so sorry you have had to wait. I told Mrs. Prosser to wake me early but my wife told her to let me sleep on. Shall we go into my study now?" He led the way down a passage, past a door marked 'Masters' Common Room', into another marked 'Headmaster'. As this door was opened, they faced a large painting of an elderly couple descending a flight of steps to a lawn. Hugo gave it a glance but was scarcely aware of its subject. He watched Martyn's hands, red from the cold, dry and slightly shaking, open a drawer.

"Here is the letter from the Ministry," said Martyn.

Hugo glanced over it, a formal notification that "following on the finds of the enquiry", the school's grant would be withdrawn.

"But what has happened?" asked Hugo, impatient to get to the more important matter of the return of his money.

Martyn sat down at his desk—slid down, rather, as though his legs had weakened beneath him and, gazing before him with an expression of profound melancholy, he said: "It was my son, Brian: my first wife's boy. He looked after the school finances. Everything was in his charge. I trusted him implicitly. He disappeared ten days ago—and every penny of the school's funds went with him."

"You mean he embezzled the money?"

"No. To put it baldly, he drew out the money and made off with it."

"But weren't the police called in?"

"Yes, but too late, I'm afraid. It was some days before we realised what had happened. He went off in the school car. He usually drove it about. It was found smashed up a mile or two this side of Crowhaven. You know there are day trips to France from there. He'd taken his passport. He must have got away from England before we even realised he'd left Ridley."

"But what was behind this? He was your son. You say you trusted him. What on earth made him do such a thing?"

"I don't know." Martyn made a movement of the utmost helplessness. "I'm as much at a loss as you are."

"There must be more to it all than this. Surely the Ministry would not withdraw its grant because your son disappeared with the school funds? That's not reasonable."

"No," Martyn agreed. "The enquiry was held before he disappeared. There had been an unfortunate friendship . . . a bit of talk among the boys . . . some gossip in Coldmouth. Then one of the parents wrote to the Ministry and eventually there was this enquiry. Statements were taken from servants—no longer employed here, needless to say—and one of the masters. It all seemed nonsense to me. I told Brian not to worry. I could not imagine anyone would take it seriously. Then he disappeared. Yesterday morning this letter came saying the grant would be withdrawn. I knew then it must all have been much more serious than I knew."

"Do you mean a friendship between your son and one of the boys?"

"Good heavens, no!" Martyn jerked up his head and stared at Hugo as though such a thing would have been unthinkable. "Brian's friendship was with someone older than himself. But . . ." he looked away, his head drooping, "does it matter who it was?"

"Did this other person disappear with your son?"

"No, he's still in Coldmouth. I've been to see him, but he says he knows nothing. Brian seems to have acted entirely on his own initiative. I must say it was very unlike him."

"I suppose it's been quite a local scandal?"

"No. Very few of the boys came from these parts. The enquiry was out of term-time and the papers were fairly discreet. Of course if Brian were caught there would be proceedings——" he looked up at Hugo. "I must expect that."

Something in the headmaster's look related the matter to Hugo in a way that made him suddenly apprehensive. He said abruptly: "Can you soon arrange the return of my money? You realise I shall have to find another place."

Martyn's mouth opened slightly. He swallowed in his throat, then said in the distant tone of extreme nervousness: "There is no money left."

It was some moments before Hugo could ask: "You mean my money has gone with the rest?"

"Everything has gone."

"I see." But he saw nothing. He felt as though a heavy weight were sinking down through his bowels. In his stunned state he was still occupied with Martyn's situation. "How are you managing now?" he asked.

"I have a small private income. Very small. I'm trying to sell the lease of this place, but it won't be easy. It's a full repairing lease, and the house is in poor shape. There are only a few more years to run. I bought it when every sort of property was at a premium. Now there's no money about." His voice faded as though it had occurred to him these worries could not interest Hugo. He tried to sound more cheerful as he added: "I must be thankful not to be completely penniless. What I have is a last remnant of my grandfather's estate."

Martyn looked up at the painting of the elderly couple, and Hugo, following his glance, met the petulant and arrogant stare with which the woman surveyed the world. As he did so, his realisation hardened. He had lost everything he had. The knowledge gave him a sudden, black satisfaction and, turning upon his reason that had always refused to see him doomed, he said: "I told you so." This was the ultimate deprivation. The triumph of the plot to keep him under.

He said dully: "But what am I to do?"

Martyn looked down at his desk: "I will pay you back when I can," he said, but he obviously had little idea when that would be.

"That won't help me now," commented Hugo, who had not even his return fare to Egypt.

"Of course you must say with us here. One more won't make much difference. We somehow manage to keep going. We have to economise, but we have Mrs. Prosser. She has been very kind. As soon as she heard what had happened, she offered to stay on. She was with my wife a long time in the old days. We can't pay her much, but she gets what we can afford, and we treat her like a friend . . ." Martyn was talking easily now, perhaps in relief that Hugo had said so little. He went on evenly, almost, it seemed to

Hugo, smugly—and in the instant of that impression Hugo began to feel resentment. Was he expected to accept his loss with a good grace? Martyn, it seemed, had lived in the world of the nicely behaved. Hugo had not. He was . . . he was being made a fool of.

Martyn was saying: "I would like you to stay. Life here is not very amusing, of course. There's not much to do. This . . . this has brought us all to a standstill, and it is difficult to see what the future holds for us." He paused, dwelling on the position in his mind, and sighed. "It is hard on you. It is very hard on my wife."

The ratio of this sympathy seemed to Hugo the last injury. He became filled with bitterness, on edge and furious that Martyn should take for granted his tame reception of the news. Looking up again at the arrogant stare of the woman in the painting, he thought: 'These people take everything for granted. They think the world is theirs.'

Aloud he said: "I suppose it is hard on your wife, but she *is* your wife; and the person to blame is your son. I'm a complete stranger. Why should I have to suffer?"

Martyn moved a hand, expressing only his inability to answer Hugo's question, but the movement turned Hugo's anger to rage. He said: "You don't seem to realise I'm practically penniless. I've not been in England since 1939. It is a strange country to me. I've given up my job in Egypt. But, anyway, even if I could be certain of finding another there, I haven't the return fare . . ."

"I might be able to raise that . . ." began Martyn, but Hugo, anguished at the thought of returning to life in Menteh without even the hope of his money to support him, broke in loudly:

49

"I'm not going back. You are not going to get rid of me so easily." Suddenly he was caught up in a blind fury, certain the money was not lost at all. No one could be such a fool as to let this thing happen. It was all a piece of roguery. He shouted: "How could your son lift out the money without your knowing? A large sum like that? The bank would have questioned it."

Martyn looked up, shocked, his face contracting in hurt surprise that shamed Hugo so that he flung himself into a sort of delirium of rage: "How do I know it isn't all a trick?"

Martyn spoke quietly: "When you see your solicitor, he will explain what has happened. As I told you, I intended writing you when you reached London. It has, I know, come as a terrible shock to you." He watched Hugo with a gentle suffering expression that Hugo found intolerable.

He spat out: "A shock! Damn you, how dare you try to patronise me! I'm the one that's been robbed. You are the one in the wrong. I want to know what you're going to do about it!"

"What can I do? At the moment there is nothing I can suggest except your staying here with us."

"I certainly mean to stay." Hugo, in an excess of nervous exhaustion, spoke calmly now, but at times he could scarcely speak at all. "I have a right to stay. You can repay the money by keeping me. I'll remain here until I feel I've had every penny of it."

Martyn nodded. "Very well. But there is no question of the money being repaid that way. It must somehow be returned to you in full."

"I'd like to know where you'll get it from."

"That is my problem." Martyn rose as he spoke. He had pulled himself together and he stood now with a dignity that seemed, in spite of all, to put Hugo in the wrong. Hugo felt chilled in a bitter and helpless exasperation from which he could find relief only by striking at the root of Martyn's self-respect. He crossed to the door and, as he opened it, he said:

"If I were you, I would look at the board in Classroom A. You may not have known what was going on, but someone evidently did."

He saw before he turned Martyn's shocked and unhappy eyes, then he went out, trying to slam the door after him. The door resisted, wheezing slowly closed, and Hugo strode through the hall and went up the stairs three at a time. As he opened the door of his room, he said aloud, dramatically. "Swindled of every penny I have. Back where I started from."

He threw himself face-down on the bed. After some minutes he tried to recreate in himself his anger's energy, but he could feel only a new emotion of regret discomforting him as it assailed his self-esteem. He knew that in the very shrillness of his anger he had stated his inferiority. Recognising that, he felt a sort of catharsis. He had humiliated no one but himself. Martyn knew the worst about him now. If he apologised, nothing need stand between them. He turned on his back and stared at the ceiling. Its scrap of pattern no longer worried him. He felt released as though he had solved a problem.

Someone knocked at the door. Feeling empty and rather light-headed, he opened it and stared at Mrs. Prosser, who was standing outside with a tray. He said vaguely: "I'm just coming down."

Mrs. Prosser looked as though she could say something pertinent if she would, but, not choosing to do so, she turned and went downstairs again.

When Hugo reached the sitting-room Martyn was standing in the middle of the room staring at the floor. He gave Hugo a quick, embarrassed glance and said: "Let us sit down." He moved to the table and Hugo, waiting with him in a strained silence, became aware of the chasm his anger had opened between them.

Mrs. Prosser brought in the food. Kyra Martyn followed her. The meal began. The silence was not broken.

Hugo, whom emotion always made hungry, had come down with an appetite. Now his appetite failed. He wanted to make some protest: to ask who had been wronged, if not he? Who in the wrong? Surely not he?

Had Martyn made a gesture of understanding now, Hugo would have rushed in with apology: "I know you are no more to blame than I." But Martyn said nothing. No one spoke. Hugo asked himself: Had he now to face, day after day, the sort of silence to which he had grown inured at his parents' table? He thought: 'What do I care? I'm used to it. They'll find they can't drive me away.'

*　　　*　　　*　　　*

Hugo's solicitors, Messrs. Cowan & Copley, had offices on the edge of Old Coldmouth. Having heard this firm named with respect during his youth, he had felt some satisfaction when in a position to employ them on his affairs.

As soon as luncheon was over, he went to a call-box on the promenade and telephoned 'young' Mr. Copley's secretary and arranged an appointment for four-thirty, the first hour at which Mr. Copley was disengaged. Then he wandered about, wretchedly restless until he had overcome the interval that separated him from his appointment. It seemed to him so unlikely that Brian Martyn could have drawn out and got away with so much money, he felt still a ghost of hope that something might be salvaged for him. Perhaps Cowan & Copley, that fabulous firm, had been cleverer than Martyn knew. Perhaps they still held Hugo's money intact.

At last he could set out for their chambers, that were in a row of early Georgian houses built for the families of senior naval officers and, as the district became commercialised, taken over gradually by professional firms. The quality of these houses, a quality that usually went unnoticed in Coldmouth, had become, for Hugo, associated with his ideas of those who had enviable, established position. He expected to find inside elegance and comfort. Instead, the waiting-room into which he was put was as drab as a vestry. He hoped for more from the junior partner's office but when, ten minutes after his arrival, 'young' Mr. Copley was free to see him, he was shown into another room as dingy as the first. His disappointment sharpened his reaction to Mr. Copley's 'professional' manner. The solicitor, a round, bald man between forty and fifty, seemed prepared to commiserate in a reserved way with his unfortunate client, but it was clear he regarded the whole occurrence as being much in the day's work.

It rushed into Hugo's mind to say: 'You were paid to

look after my interests,' but he swallowed this back and said in a tone no more than coldly unimpressed by Copley's preamble:

"I am at a loss to understand how this business has been carried out. Brian Martyn did not embezzle the money. He simply drew it out and made off with it. Does the bank permit the secretary of a concern like Ridley School to empty an account without explanation?"

Copley moved round in his chair and, propping his left elbow on its back and his head on his left hand, he stretched out his right arm and fingered the pens and pencils on his desk. With an air of incongruous aloofness, his eyelids drooping over his eyes, he described in measured tones what had happened.

"Young Martyn certainly showed ingenuity," he said. "More, apparently, than his friends would have given hm credit for. I suspect he had the whole business planned a good while. When we examined the books—six months ago now—the school was solvent. Comfortably so. Not what we'd call a gold-mine, but a going concern; a nice investment for a teacher with a little cash. We'd no reason to suppose the situation would change. This fellow, Brian Martyn, as soon as we declared ourselves satisfied, started drawing out regular sums—for alterations and improvements at the school, he said. New man coming, place needs money spending on it, etc., etc. No harm in that. Eventually all the capital was drawn out; then, on the security of the money due from you, the bank let him have an overdraft. The manager seems to have had a high opinion of the Martyns. Charles Martyn comes from a good family and had inherited a small private income. He had taken out a fairly considerable overdraft when the school first opened and paid it off all right." Copley flicked up his eyelids an instant to glance at Hugo, then he turned, somewhat wearily, in his chair. "Well, the long and the short of it is—your money paid off the overdraft."

"I see." Hugo nodded slowly, then suddenly burst out: "But why? Why should I be the loser rather than the bank? They made the mistake of allowing the overdraft. Why should they be justified in seizing the money of an outsider to pay their losses?"

Copley's expression remained unchanged. "The answer is," he replied evenly, "you were not an outsider. As soon as you signed the agreement you became as liable as Martyn."

"If you'd held up the transfer a bit, the bank would have had to whistle for its money."

"We were in no position to foresee what would happen. But, even had the transfer been held up and you refused to pay the money over, the result would have merely been a court case. You might have landed yourself with heavy costs into the bargain." Copley, now gazing at his finger-nails, seemed to exude self-satisfaction. To Hugo his attitude proclaimed that the law was the law, an admirable thing, and he its admirable exponent.

Hugo told himself that the members of this old, respected firm of solicitors were a pack of fools. He would have been glad of the relief of accusing someone, but he knew that to accuse Copley would be a waste of time.

He said in his hardest tone: "You all seem perfectly satisfied that I should carry the can back. Brian Martyn's made his get-away. All right! But how about the father?

55

What do we know of him? How can we be sure the Martyns did not arrange all this between them?"

This time Copley was shocked into sitting upright. His answer terminated the interview: "I am certain Mr. Charles Martyn is an honourable man." He stood up, not offering Hugo his hand, and said: "I have another client waiting. You can be sure, Mr. Fletcher, we have done all possible on your behalf. Good afternoon."

Hugo went. He was the loser: he was in the right: yet, here, too, he had been treated like a culprit. In his disgust he was half prepared to pack and leave Coldmouth and never communicate with any of them again. But why should he? Why on earth should he hand over his fortune for a gesture? He'd done something like that once before, and he'd done it then for the first and last time. Now, whatever happened, he would sit it out.

With all the time in the world to waste, he started to walk back to Ridley. He felt a certain morose calm in the knowledge there was nothing to hope for. There was nothing to be done about things. He was back at the beginning again.

Knowing himself committed to Coldmouth, whether he liked it or not, he began to look about him with different eyes. He could no longer despise the significance of every road and corner. The memories he had rejected before, now put themselves squarely in his path. Humble in his new impoverishment, he let them over-ride him.

He took the road through the ruined High Street and stopped at a wide corner of gravel that marked the sweep of a past pavement. A broken-down paling rimmed the pit where Webley's department store had stood. Nothing memorable remained but the lamp-post on the opposite pavement against which he used to lean while he waited for Tilly to finish work.

Tilly had had almost no friends in Coldmouth when Hugo first met her. She had grown up in Brighton and, when her mother died, had come here to live with an aunt. Her looks and manner had got her a job at Webley's as soon as she applied. Webley's was advertised as the largest department store on the south coast. Perhaps it was. Anyway, it was regarded in Coldmouth as a 'superior' shop and only 'superior' girls could find employment there, but Tilly had not been merely superior in the Coldmouth sense. She had been, indeed, a charmer. When Hugo first asked her to go with him to the Gala Café, she jumped at the invitation as though she had never in her life before been invited anywhere. That, he soon learnt, was a trick of hers. She was not an amusing girl, not very clever, but she somehow conveyed that the company of every person she met, man or woman, was a delight to her. Hugo's mother, always a fool, had said at once: "That's the girl for you," as though Hugo, with scarcely the price of a cinema seat on him, could pick and choose among all the girls in Coldmouth.

From the first he had never supposed Tilly meant to waste much time on him. He expected her to give him up as soon as she made other friends. Like a man with catastrophe hanging over him, he so dreaded her loss that he almost wished to suffer it and get it over. He also wished she would go sooner than later, and he felt at times an odd impatience at the fact that she remained.

After he had stared a while into the lost shop's great basement, he crossed the road and propped himself against the lamp-post as he had propped himself night after night for seven months in the past. The iron seemed worn by his shoulder, or perhaps his shoulder was worn by the iron: whatever the reason, he seemed to slide at once into an habitual stance. Looking back on that last winter in England, the winter before the war, he felt his life had been squandered here as, in the darkness and cold, he wished time away.

The shop closed at six, but there was always some reason why Tilly could not leave punctually; sales and stock-taking, Christmas or Easter, a difficult customer or trouble over accounts. While he waited, it was as though his whole consciousness concentrated itself to a point of longing that the next person to come out through the doors should be she. Yet, when at last she appeared and ran eagerly across to him, he would respond with a peevish shrug of his shoulders. He felt bound to try her to the utmost, to force her to revolt against him, so that when the separation came, as he was sure it must come, he could claim the fault was his.

He was certain that, secretly, beneath her sweet for-bearance with her poor share of fortune, she was as am-bitious as he to climb out of the littleness of Coldmouth. As for himself—what he had most desired was the con-fidence of being unassailable. In Coldmouth there was a point at which certain people—those of exceptional social position or attainments—were above criticism. "Oh, well, people like that, of course! What do you expect!" His desire was not to change himself but to change his status, but he knew that nothing he did here would reassess him. He would have to go away. One day he would go away; but how, where or to do what, he did not know. Only the necessity was there and because of it he feared not only to lose her, but not to lose her. If she remained, might she not hamper him when the moment came for his escape?

The last evening he waited here had been during the winter sales. He had stood for more than an hour. The shop was crowded with women. When he took up his stand he could see the shop-walkers struggling to get the doors closed. Once the bolts were dropped no one could get in, but the customers inside would not leave. The bitches!

The iron black of the night was overlaid with fog. The cold was painful. Leaning against the lamp-post, his old raincoat pulled about him, his hands in his pockets, he cursed her because she did not walk out on the lot of them.

He had to wait where he was. If he walked around, he might miss her when she did come out. He could not go to the Gala because that would entail spending money he must keep to spend with her. He stood unmoving, damning her and longing for her.

When, almost the last, she pushed through the staff door and ran to him crying: "Hugo, Hugo, I thought I should never get away," he made no sign. As she crossed the road she opened her arms and, when she reached him, she flung them round him—then she gasped and drew back. She said: "You're frozen. The cold seems to be coming from you."

He said in a voice as cold as his flesh: "Are you surprised?" and, glancing down at his body, he seemed to see an icy humidity rise from it. He stood, frozen against the lamp-post, until she let her hands drop from him and said as though she were to blame: "I'm sorry I've been so long."

"It doesn't matter." He jerked himself into motion and stumped stiffly beside her down the side street to the promenade.

She said: "It's pay day. Let's go and have something to eat."

Because he knew she could not afford to pay for a restaurant meal, he felt the more angry and irritated at the offer. He said: "I'm not hungry."

"What's the matter?"

"Nothing."

"You do seem cross."

"Do I?" he bit off his replies with a self-dramatising irony, lifted above himself by anger so that he wanted only to be free and alone.

While he was visualising freedom from everything that made his life here, he noticed a man come from the car park at the end of the road and walk towards them. It was Cyril Webley, the richest young man in Coldmouth, eldest son of the great man who had built up the shop where Tilly worked and was now one of its directors and chief shareholders. Hugo thought: 'If I were Cyril Webley, Tilly would not keep me waiting for an hour and a half,' and he felt in a supernormal area of understanding the magnificence that would be Tilly's were she Webley's girl and not his.

It was then he was caught in a sort of crazy inspiration. As Webley came up to them, Hugo did what he could not have done at any other moment of his life. He put out a hand to pause him, and Webley paused, surprised. They had barely known one another at school. Webley, two years Hugo's senior, had been head boy and captain of cricket. Now he was a power in Coldmouth. He was a solicitor employed by his father's company, and would one day inherit his father's shares in it.

Webley smiled, willing enough to be friendly. He had always been a good chap, modest and much liked.

"Here!" Hugo caught his arm and pushed him at Tilly. "Let me introduce you to my girl friend. She works in your shop. She's the best girl in the world. She deserves someone better than me." As he said this he glanced at Tilly as though he were saying: 'There, that's the man you'd like, isn't it? but you're not likely to get him: not that one: so perhaps you'll be content with me.'

Cyril Webley, sharing Tilly's embarrassment, looked at her with sympathy and sympathy's admiration, then, with his goodwill and good-humour, he tried to put the situation right. "Isn't he a crazy chap?" He smiled at Tilly as though no one could be annoyed by anyone as crazy as Hugo.

Hugo swept out his arm: "I feel you two were made for one another and now, having brought you together . . ." he bowed elaborately, "I'll leave you to get to know one another," and he turned on his heel and strode back to the High Street. His feeling of triumph had been such, his feet felt winged.

There was a silence behind him, then Tilly called distressfully: "Hugo! Come back. You can't leave me like this."

"Oh, can't I?" he quickened his steps against the possibility of pursuit, then, dodging round a corner, he began to run, elated by the fantasy of his own behaviour.

It was as though he had given some great performance on a stage—but more than that. More, more, he had been creator of the scene, not interpreter. He existed in the applause of his enthusiasm. He went home and, as though

61

drunk, dropped on his bed and slept. Even the next morning he was content, seeming, with a gesture, to have released some fury from himself. To add to the dramatic effect of the gesture, he did not telephone Tilly at the shop or go near her: he kept out of sight, not only of her but of everyone he knew. He imagined he was being discussed among them for this latest escapade. A crazy fellow. He imagined Tilly's uneasy bewilderment at it all.

During this time, strangely enough, it did not occur to him that anything could come of his introducing Webley to Tilly. Tilly was a pretty girl, a kindly, generous, charming girl, but the fact she had been his girl must have devalued her in Coldmouth eyes. More than that, Cyril was not confined to Coldmouth circles. He moved in a sort of aristocracy of money that controlled the whole of the south-east coast. He would not be likely to marry a Coldmouth girl.

A week later, thinking he had been out of sight long enough, Hugo visited the Gala Café. It was then he saw Tilly and Cyril, with fingers linked, go out to the dancing floor. The mechanism of his body seemed to pause a moment. He gaped in realisation of the incredible folly of having introduced them. That the folly had been his own made him feel the more wronged.

Yet, even though the man was Cyril Webley, even though he sensed their intimacy, some wild hope of regaining her propelled him to their table as soon as they sat down again.

This time Webley's smile was a smile of discomfort. 'Probably heard all about my misdeeds by now,' thought Hugo, who put on a grotesque air of confidence and said to Tilly:

"How about having a dance with an old friend?"

62

Tilly did not smile. She managed to look as though he were meaningless to her. She spoke with a quiet, unrelenting uninterest: "No, thank you, Hugo."

Both of them looked away from him, yet he could not leave them. Grinning and ignored, he said: "That's a nice way to treat a pal. Aren't you going to thank me for bringing you together?"

Still he was ignored, and, after a terrible minute, he laughed, waved a hand at them and went off with a jaunty air that got him through the door and out of sight. No further. On the pavement, standing in the wind from the sea, he felt he no longer had reason for living.

Even now, twelve years after, staring at the remnants of Webley's shop, he felt like a mortal chill the touch of the desolation of that night. Could he ever be so unhappy again? Never, never. Such unhappiness inoculated one against itself.

As he turned and went on down the devastated High Street, he wondered: Supposing he had walked into the sea that night, would he have missed much? The twelve, or was it thirteen, years that had passed had merely brought him back to where he started. But his life had not ended that night—and it was not ended now. As he thought of his present situation, a look, obstinate and wild, came into his face. He was chiefly conscious of Charles Martyn's disapproval of him. And what did he care? What the hell did he care? The Martyns meant nothing to him. Whatever they had been in the past (and, he supposed, Kyra had had her day), what were they now but a middle-aged couple becoming elderly in obscurity? In short, they were done for. Written off. Finished.

While he—he was still young enough to fight. He had always had to fight. Remembering that, a black, inner belligerency took hold of him and was, for a while, so sharp-tasting and venomous, he could have struck a blow at some innocent passer-by; then it receded, leaving him in a muddle of memories of his long conflict with life in this place.

He had started to pass out of the bombed area into a sort of border country of houses part-whole and part-ruined, among which stood a cinema—no, only the façade, with a doorway of spotted chromium that still held in its frame a few splinters of pink looking-glass. Beyond was emptiness. Above the door was a board from which hung strips of posters. Above that a maze of crumpled wiring that had once held neon tubes.

He remembered the blaze of that neon turning about his eyes as the car made its arc across the road. It was the shock of the accident—no, not of the accident, but of the injustice that followed it—that had given him freedom to walk out on all the claims of his life.

The night of the accident, a spring night, he had spent as usual at the Gala Café watching for Tilly and Cyril. He did not expect them. Going to the Gala at all must have been Tilly's idea, for Webley had never been seen there before. For the first month of their friendship they danced there perhaps twice a week, so Hugo had held to the ridiculous hope that Tilly was simply taking Cyril there that he might see them together. Why, after all, should they go to the Gala when they could have gone to the Royal Beach or the Bristol, or driven to one of the big coastal road-houses? If she came for his sake, then . . . then, it was like a retort in a squabble, a response, a contact; the situation was alive. Perhaps, after all, it was he whom she wanted. She was merely teaching him a lesson.

But they came less and less frequently. Two and three weeks passed before they reappeared; two months passed and the winter was breaking. Soon the town would take on its summer life. The Gala would be crowded with visitors. Three months passed. It was May. Hugo had seen neither Tilly nor Cyril for three months, yet with gloomy delectation he sat there every night and watched the couples making their entrances up the stairs. As a sort of penance for being himself, he gave up smoking at that time, so he had more money to spend, but not very much. He had still to get through most of each evening warding off with his will the enquiries of those bitchy little waitresses: "Anything else you'll be wanting?" When the answer was "No," the chit was slapped down on the table and the girl would retire to lean against a post and stare you away from a table that might in your absence be taken by someone who would leave a tip. More than once he had been made to overhear the exclamation: "Oh, Lord, I've got Peter the Pauper at my table again." He had not found it a world in which the poor pitied the poor. But he had not asked for pity, he had asked for what he got—that ironical pretence at politeness.

That night, the night of the accident, the Gala, which did not close until eleven o'clock, had been invaded by the rugger team, victorious and drunk, at a loose end after the bars closed at half-past ten. At once they had taken the place over, sprawling at the tables, shouting across the dance floor, or jumping down to it and seizing the prettiest girls from their partners. The girls had added to the row by giggling shrilly or inviting the attention of all by loud indignation.

Hugo, sitting aloof in the emptier reaches of the café, waiting to be defensively offensive if attacked, had been completely disarmed by 'Quids-in' Lawson's pausing at his table and saying "Hello."

"Hello," said Hugo and 'Quids-in' suddenly fell into the chair beside him. As he sat he muttered words that sounded like:

"Sick of that lot."

Hugo dared not reply for fear of saying the wrong thing, but he stared at 'Quids-in' with a sympathy that had in it a sort of love. 'Quids-in' was the same age as Hugo, but he looked forty. His face, a mauvish-red in colour, looked wizened as though with extreme cold, and his little brown eyes dodged about in their sockets with what might have been mad indignation. Hugo's pleasure became almost ecstatic as he realised 'Quids-in' was indeed expressing a grievance against his fellow rugger men. It was scarcely conceivable that that powerful, patrician force could be split by grievance, or that one of its members should choose an outsider like Hugo in whom to confide, yet all this, apparently, had happened.

Hugo, pushing his gratification from sight as best he could, tried to speak as man to man: "What's the trouble, 'Quids-in', old chap?"

But 'Quids-in' could make no clear statement. He mumbled: "Put it there himself, damn the lot of them. Said I trod on his f—— what-not. I don't know. Makes me sick." He caught at the arm of a passing waitress and

66

whispered: "Bring double Scotch," but the bar was closed. He could have nothing but light refreshments.

"There you are, you see!" 'Quids-in' fixed Hugo with a look significant and suffering. Suddenly he thumped the table and shouted: "Damn the lot of them!"

One of the team bawled over to him: "Go it, 'Quids-in', break up the happy home."

'Quids-in' smiled inanely and waved like a baby from a perambulator, but when he looked back at Hugo he became glum again, saying darkly: "That's the one."

"That one over there?" Hugo kept the conversation going in the hope the story would come out in the end, but nothing came. 'Quids-in's' mumblings had almost died down when suddenly, as though jolted into clarity by a revelation, he sat upright and said aloud:

"You're not really a bad chap, Fletcher. They can say what they like, but I've always said you're not really a bad chap."

Hugo looked down at the dregs of his coffee. He was, as he was expected to be, flattered. 'Quids-in', his magnanimity increased by his magnanimity, slapped down his hand again and said: "Going home?"

"Yes, soon," Hugo agreed, eager to remain in this desirable company.

"Come on, then. Give you a lift."

'Quids-in' got up unsteadily and, followed by Hugo, made a regal departure, smiling about him and waving to his friends, who called after him: "Good old 'Quids-in'."

On the stairs he stopped and pulled out a flask-shaped bottle with a little whisky at the bottom. "Have a drink," he said, pushing it at Hugo. Hugo shook his head and 'Quids-in' drained the bottle and tossed it over his shoulder. "Finished. Pity. Drive best when I'm tight."

Seated at the wheel of his small car, 'Quids-in' fumbled with the gears until Hugo thought something was wrong with them; but, to his surprise, 'Quids-in' dropped his head on to the wheel and whimpered: "Can't do it."

"I'll get you home," said Hugo. He had no driving licence and did not drive well, but he felt his part now to be an heroic one. He persuaded 'Quids-in' to make the difficult effort of changing seats, then, with a crunch of gears, he started the car and got them safely away from the esplanade into the High Street. The Lawsons had a house on the downs outside Ridley. The High Street, as they turned into it, stretched away black, glossy and deserted, beneath a long row of central lights, but as they approached Ridley, the doors of a cinema opened and suddenly the pavements and road were crowded. 'Quids-in' had been slumped in a stupor, but this movement about him roused him and with a yell of "Pass, you blithering idiot," he flung himself on the wheel and turned it with maniac strength and determination. The car swung in a rapid circle through the crowd, bowling people to right and left. When they crashed to a standstill among the shattered glass of the cinema doors, 'Quids-in' took the force of the concussion. Hugo, masked by his body, was unhurt. At first Hugo's only concern was for his companion, whose head had hit the windscreen, and who now lay with his neck askew. He was loosening 'Quids-in's' collar when someone rapped on the car window and angrily ordered him to get out and see what he had done.

A girl of thirteen was beneath the rear wheels: a girl

68

whom, Hugo thought when they got her out, should have been at home in bed. Instead she had gone alone, unknown to her parents, to the second house of the cinema. She died three hours later in hospital. 'Quids-in', his neck broken, was already dead. Hugo, who had been in the driver's seat when the car crashed, was the natural culprit. The whole rugger team lined up at the inquest to testify that 'Quids-in' was a splendid chap—"the salt of the earth," one of them had called him—who had had no more than a couple of beers all evening. Old Lawson had wept in the court-room and the coroner had spoken sternly to Hugo, telling him he would do his case little good by trying to impose on to a dead friend responsibility for this 'dastardly piece of driving.'

And here again was the pink glass door, shattered this time not by 'Quids-in's' car but by bombs. Hugo turned his back on it and hurried on up the High Street, but, remembering that when he reached Ridley he would have nothing to do, he loitered again, giving himself to his thoughts.

Had it been in the coroner's power to condemn him, he would have been condemned on the spot. And, Hugo realised as he looked about him, it was not only the coroner that stood his enemy. In one pair of eyes after another he met a condemnation that came less from friendship for 'Quids-in' as from hatred for himself. Something in the atmosphere at the inquest was naked and declared: he recognised it for an eagerness to damn him. Hugo was stupefied. He could not understand it, but he felt himself done for.

During the weeks that passed before the Crowhaven

Assizes, he was treated as though judgment had already been given against him. Yet he was acquitted.

With no thanks to Tilly.

Her evidence, like that of three other witnesses brought at Old Lawson's expense to Crowhaven, was voluntarily given. They were all people whom he had upset in some way or other. They came to testify that he was subject to fits of irrational behaviour.

Remembering Tilly in the witness-box, Hugo caught his breath painfully. He suffered still as, a thousand times in the past, he had suffered whenever his unguarded thoughts stubbed themselves against that memory.

When she was called to give her evidence, she had given Hugo one brief, sad glance, then did not look in his direction again. She was moist-eyed, obviously nervous; she spoke very quietly.

'During her association with the accused, had his behaviour led her to regard him as a person of erratic temperament?'

"Yes," she trembled as though at any moment she would break down.

'Would she, in her own words, describe to the jury any incident,' etc., etc.

She described two or three small incidents that were each acclaimed by the Crown counsel as proof of Hugo's irrationality. She did not make public what would have been more to the point—the story of the evening he pushed her into Webley's arms. Hugo knew it was in her mind all the time. That was the incident his guilt would nullify. A man mad enough to run a car into a crowd of people would be mad enough to hand her over to someone else. That was clear. Had she told that story the jury might have agreed with her. As it was, the jury were not convinced. Perhaps it sensed the truth in his defence. There was also the fact he had been proved sober when tested after the accident by the police (thank heaven he had not accepted 'Quids-in's' offer of a drink!). In the end he was pronounced not guilty of manslaughter.

When he went with his mother to pay the fine imposed on him for driving without a licence, he saw Lawson standing with a group of newspaper men and heard him say: "My only wish was to vindicate my dead son."

'But they had no choice,' he told himself as he passed the busy shops of Ridley High Street. 'They had to set me free.'

His freedom then was more than freedom to pass from the court-house into the white, thin sunlight of early summer. It was freedom to escape from Coldmouth altogether. Shock had cut him off from fear.

He was, it seemed, the incurable defaulter. No jury could exonerate him here. He could only take himself from Coldmouth's sight.

When he went, he went for good: or so he thought. Until he saw Martyn's advertisement there had been no question of his return. Why that had swept him up in sudden eagerness to come back here, he did not know. The wish to disconcert Tilly was, at the most, the symbol of a reason. The reason itself, if there was one, might be contained in a knot of anguish in his mind's recess where his consciousness flickered, always avoiding contact, like a tongue tip over the exposed nerve of a tooth. What was there? A knot where a branch had been lopped? He could

71

not tell. It was too painful to be examined more closely: he would ignore it if he could.

He put the past from his thoughts. He had suffered enough of it for one day. He went on to Ridley House and the silent supper table.

CHAPTER III

THE next morning was wet. He had almost forgotten rain. Although he now had no money to spare, he knew he would have to buy an overcoat of some kind if he were not to spend half the winter prisoner in the house.

When the sky cleared, he went to a Government surplus store in the back streets behind the harbour and bought a raincoat. He wore it from the shop. Looking at his reflection in windows as he passed, he saw himself changed by his cheap and skimpy coat into a person of a poorer class, into the poor elementary school-teacher who had to wear an outgrown schoolboy's coat, a creature without style or substance, hurt, impotent and vainly revengeful.

He bought a newspaper and went to the buffet of the Harbour Station for a cup of tea. There he stretched as far as he could the excitements of the *Coldmouth Evening Chronicle*: 'The engagement of Miss Jocey Clark, daughter of Mr. H. T. Q. Clark, the well-known Coldmouth jeweller . . .'; 'Speech by Sir Cecil Plumstead, Conservative Candidate for Coldmouth East'; 'The Old Coldmouth Billiards' Contest . . .'

Nothing now to compare with 'Local Youth to stand trial for Manslaughter. "Dastardly Driving," says Coroner. Today Hugo Fletcher, son of a retired naval officer residing at 16, Henley Street, Old Coldmouth . . .'

73

Vividly his father's dark and narrow face came into his mind. As Hugo watched it the heavy skin-folds, running from nose to chin, were pushed out by a smile that was like the grimace of someone who had swallowed strychnine—a retired naval officer who had ruined himself and brought his family into poverty and gave only one explanation to the world: "I married a fool."

Hugo never understood why his mother, who must have been a plump, pretty, jolly girl, had chosen this sombre man. She had been the daughter of a doctor, her father's adored only child, inheritor of his house and fortune; while her husband had been an orphan brought up by grandparents who had sacrificed themselves that he might enter the Navy as a cadet. His grandmother had fulfilled her ambition of living until she saw him an officer—an officer with nothing but his pay, poor wretch! She had not lived to see him marry so well. But his wife's money had not been enough to recompense him for those days when he had dreaded his mess-bills and had felt sick at the sight of a subscription list. Hugo was certain of that. How, otherwise, could he explain that interlude in his father's sober, hard-working, joyless life? An interlude of madness, when he and two other officers in his mess had become possessed (there was no other word to describe their frenzy of investment and visions of fortune) by the prospectuses of a financier who had ended his career with a long prison sentence.

Like most naval men, they were innocents on dry land. They believed that, could they find the money to invest at the right moment, an immense fortune must result. All fortunes, they were sure, were made that way: simply by having the money when the opportunity of investment came. Mr. Fletcher had not only gambled with his own savings; he had talked his wife into letting him have the fifteen thousand pounds her father had left her. (How often Hugo had heard her mourn that fifteen thousand pounds.) More than that he had borrowed from friends, money-lenders and anyone who could be persuaded to lend.

Hugo wondered if the sudden, indeed overnight, collapse of the whole dream had not left his father a little demented.

It happened at a time when the Navy was being cut down. Commanders like his father, men in early middle age, were being induced by the offer of bonuses to retire on small pensions. Mr. Fletcher accepted retirement and commuted half his pension. All the money in hand went to the money-lenders. (One of the three officers, a man named Esher, had committed suicide, and Mr. Fletcher, when in one of his very rare good moods, would say with grim humour: "Esher's the only man I ever knew who got the better of the money-lenders.") The other creditors were paid off over the years. These debts, which he threw up to his wife and son as though they had been the borrowers, were desolation to them all. It took nearly twenty years to pay them off. Remembering those years, Hugo was sure the creditors themselves would not have oppressed and underfed a mother and child as Mr. Fletcher oppressed and underfed his wife and son on his creditors' behalf.

Another man might have made the best of the situation by taking a small flat in East Coldmouth or a cottage on the downs—such things were not out of reach in those days—and finding a job to add to the half-pension. It is true they were lean times for job-seekers but others worked and lived well enough. Not Mr. Fletcher. Faced with misfortune, he behaved as though he would spite his situation by exaggerating it. He took out a mortgage on a four-roomed workman's cottage in Henley Street, an area of respectable gloom. . . .

A door slammed.

Hugo, startled out of his thoughts, found the waitress locking up. She had put a 'Closed' notice on the buffet counter. Hugo was the last customer. He gulped down his cold tea. The waitress unbolted the door for him and, when he went, rebolted it upon his heels.

Twilight was falling. The harbour water had turned to ink: there was a chill unwelcome in the light. As he walked down the platform he could hear the sea slapping about beneath the boards.

The Old Coldmouth bus was standing by the kerb. This was the time of day when, coming from the Teachers' Training College, he would pass the waiting bus and walk the two miles home to tea. Now he stepped aboard it.

The driver and conductor were sitting smoking inside and carrying on a conversation of monosyllables and grunts. The conductor's face had for Hugo a remote familiarity, too remote to be placed, yet he felt stabbed by annoyance at it. He took the front seat to be away from the platform. Almost as soon as he had sat down, the driver went round to his cabin and the bus started. The conductor, whistling through his front teeth and giving a slap to the seat backs as he passed them, came up to the front of the bus where Hugo was sitting. There he bent and looked out of the window as though there was some meaning for him in the blankness of the passing dockyard wall.

"Days drawing in," he said.

After Hugo had agreed the conductor made a dip with his body, gave a sort of inward laugh of satisfaction and said: "Name of Fletcher, isn't it? You don't remember me. Recognised you at once."

Hugo looked at the long face with the out-hanging lips and eyes brown and globular as the eyes of a hare, and he moved uneasily. "I don't remember you." His tone and face were expressionless, but his impulse was to put up a hand to protect himself.

The conductor, still grinning, repeated the dip of his body and said easily: "Well, it was years ago. We were at Whittaker Road School," and his grin broadened.

Hugo, realising the man meant no harm, made an effort to pull himself together. He smiled, so the conductor said eagerly: "You got a scholarship to the Grammar. I remember. What did you do after that?"

"I didn't go to the Grammar School. I went to St. Aubyn's."

"Oh, top of the list, were you?" The conductor sounded as though there were something comic about it all. "And now you're a big bug, I suppose?"

"I became a teacher."

"A teacher!" Condescension came into his manner now; he shook his head. "Indoor work. Wouldn't suit me. I like the buses."

"You see life."

"That's right." He gave a sudden wild squawk of laughter and went noisily back to the platform. The bus stopped; some people got on; the conductor gave the bell handle a heavy down flip with the palm of his hand. Several minutes later he returned and, leaning over Hugo, he whispered hoarsely: "*Life!* You see it in the raw!" After which, roaring with laughter, he clattered up the stairs. He was still up there, loudly singing, when Hugo got off the bus.

Pausing on the kerb and lighting a cigarette, Hugo found his fingers were trembling. He felt shamed as though he had come ignominiously from the hands of a tormentor—yet, in fact, he had suffered no more than a brush with an old insecurity.

'Don't behave like a fool,' he told himself as he struck into Coldmouth's hinterland.

Brought here for the first time at the age of eight, he had been amazed that anyone could choose to leave a house with a garden and a swing and a radio-gramophone, a house near the sea, for a dark, little inland cottage with no garden at all. He said: "But why have we come here, Mummy? *Why?*"

"Because we have no money."

He had lived for a long time in a sort of dream of the other house and the wonders he had taken for granted there —the swing, the hammock, the car, the radio-gramophone (a rare and expensive thing in those days), and the girl called Nannie who had taken him for walks.

At his new school in Whittaker Road he had talked innocently of his past opulence, expecting the children there to be as entranced by his memories as he was himself. They did not believe him. He struck enmity like a flint. It flashed back at him. He was called a liar, a boaster, someone who thought himself better than his fellows. Hugo had never met anything like this before. He was bewildered.

The father of one of the boys, hearing of Hugo's claims,

declared him to be a 'bloody little snob' and this was at
once repeated among the other accusations: "My dad says
you're a bloody little snob. You and your radio-
gramophone! He says you've never seen one in your life."

"We had one. We had one!" Hugo, protesting, came
near to tears, then was horribly backed up by an unpopular
boy called Vernon, who said:

"My dad's got one, too. It's a big, round thing with two
little pieces of wood sticking out, and one's got his name
on."

"That's not a radio-gramophone," shouted Hugo,
attacking with hatred his sole supporter, "you haven't got
one. You're a liar, but I'm not lying. We did have one.
We did."

No one liked Vernon, yet they rallied to him, asking
couldn't his father own a radio-gramophone as well as
Hugo's? If Hugo had ever had one, where was it now?

"Come on, take us along to your house and show us."

But there was no radio-gramophone at Henley Street.

Of all the boys at Whittaker Road School, Vernon alone
remained with a name in Hugo's memory, for he had been
an insidious enemy, one that pretended sympathy to make
Hugo talk, then, behind his back, exaggerated into scan-
dalous shape everything he said. Hugo, in his loneliness,
could not resist Vernon's company. Though he would, if
asked, have said he hated Vernon, yet there was a sort of
intoxication in confiding in him. Vernon, for his part,
seemed drawn to Hugo's solitude. When they were together,
they seemed to be bound in understanding, yet Vernon
could never resist the advantage to be gained by betraying
Hugo. The periods of their intimacy always ended with

Hugo's being waylaid and attacked by a crowd: "Vernon says you think yourself better than us. He says you wouldn't go to Whittaker Road if you could help it. You think you ought to be at a posh school. Your mother and father are really posh, aren't they? They just got poor by accident, didn't they?" And Hugo, with his back against a wall, got his nose and ears tweaked, his ankles kicked, his stomach punched, as one hand after another came out of the imprisoning semi-circle of boys.

At these times Vernon, of course, kept out of sight; and Hugo hated him as he had never hated anyone or anything in his life before.

In every book about a school bully which Hugo borrowed from the public library there would be a noble older boy who, recognising truth in the wronged child, would stand forth as his champion. Hugo would cry over these stories, longing for such a friend, but no one championed him. Until he was strong and quick-witted enough to turn aggressor, he was the most bullied child in Old Coldmouth. He could do or say nothing right. He had a certain timidity that he overcame and, strangely, by this overcoming became virulent. Yet, knowing himself timid within, he was the more conscious of injustice.

It had been less ambition than need to escape Whittaker Road School that had kept him working for a scholarship. He would have worked as hard to escape his home had escape been possible, but he knew he would not escape home before he escaped childhood.

Remembering this, he turned the last corner and faced Henley Street. There it was, still intact. Intact and unchanged. The little, flat-fronted, dark-brick houses, lacking the usual scraps of front garden, were exposed to the street. His eyes passed over one familiar yellow-brown door after another until he paused on the most familiar of them: number sixteen, yellow-brown like the rest. He had once watched his father paint it, then grain it with a steel comb. Mr. Fletcher when he left the Service had taken up house-painting as a hobby and had bought pots of treacly paint, dark green, dark brown and rusty red, from a petty officer who smuggled them out from the dockyard store.

This door had once been his only refuge from his class-mates, yet if, on coming to it, he would hear his father shouting inside or his mother crying, he would choose rather the fearful street. He was frightened of his father, but his mother troubled him most. He dreaded the anguish which would come into her voice when she saw him, her child and ally.

"Oh, there you are, Hugo, my darling, my only one! You are away all day. You don't know what I have to suffer here alone with him," and Hugo, in his effort to share her suffering, would feel as though his heart would burst. It was true he could escape to school and, as though his escape were a desertion, he was filled with guilt. His helplessness was unbearable. He could only say:

"When I'm grown up, I'll take you away from him. We'll go away together."

Standing now at the end of Henley Street, unwilling to enter into it and pass the door of number sixteen, he heard the oncoming of a group of boys who came up to him and threw themselves past him as though he did not exist. Their every sound and movement was familiar to him. It was amazing that his size and age could put him out of their reach. He watched after them as they went bawling down the street. Nothing had changed.

When he was a child Hugo had scarcely noticed the street noises; his mother had thought them friendly. It was his father who had complained of life brushing the window and trespassing on the doorstep. When the boys, loud-voiced, given to hoots and howls and outbursts of brawling, trudged down the road thumping shoulders against doors and windows, or made screeching noises into letter boxes, Mr. Fletcher would stir and mutter: "No privacy here, no privacy, no privacy at all!"; and when the neighbours, curious about the Fletchers, would peer in through the chintz curtains (in those days everyone else preferred lace), his father would scowl at them and say aloud: "Nosey Parkers. Always wanting to know your business."

Hugo walked down the road. On the first corner was the newsagent-tobacconist who sold cheap sweets; on the furthest corner, the public-house. When he reached his old home, Hugo turned automatically and saw in the window the bone frigate his father had made during the first year of his retirement. He recognised it at once—the ship he had never been allowed to touch; the only one his father made, because to make one, and that perfect, was enough. But the curtains had changed. The exhausted-looking chintz had gone and now there was orange casement cloth exactly like that in the windows on either side.

With a pang he saw, among the puce-red bricks, the two bricks that had a dark blue sheen on them. Immortal bricks! Hugo got past quickly, then crossed the road and returned on the other side. Now, from a safer distance, he gazed at the house, half expecting it to make some sign to him, but it gazed back without recognition.

Was it possible his father was still alive? Despite the fact he had scarcely given him a thought during their separation, he was depressed by his picture of the old man existing through the years in the old routine of protective respectability. On an impulse of pity, he went over and knocked at the door.

There was an immediate movement inside the house that caused Hugo's heart to thump, but the movement apparently was only preparation for opening the door and a full minute elapsed before footsteps came down the hall. Even then— a pause. The door opened. A thin, little woman put her nose and eye round its edge.

"Is Mr. Fletcher at home?" Hugo asked.

"Who are you?"

"His son."

At that the woman looked out, not at Hugo, but at the street, then she gave her head a jerk: "You'd better come in."

After she had closed the door, she marched ahead of him to the back room. Hugo, with a shock of remembrance, sniffed the smell of the house. Once, trying to define it to himself, he had decided it was like a mixture of stale biscuits, linoleum and cooking-fat, but there was added to it some other smell that made it unique in the world. With it there came back to him acutely the claustrophobia it used to produce in him. Nothing in the back room had changed. In the last steel colour of the evening light he could see the floor was covered with the same yellow and green linoleum polished so that the printed pattern was nearly gone. In the centre of the room stood the same square table and four chairs, and round the walls, so close one could scarcely move from the table without knocking against them, the sideboard, the green plush sofa and the table with the wireless set.

Somehow his mother's untidiness had made the place tolerable. Now it had the cold, cleaned, polished, antiseptic look of a corner in an institute. There was no fire. He could tell from the copy of *True Love Stories* lying face-down on a chair that the woman had been reading by the window to save the gas-light.

Outside the window was the small backyard with the outdoor privy and the walls green with damp. Hugo's old bicycle, rusted and tyreless, still hung there on two hooks on the wall.

The woman waited until Hugo turned to her, then, with a slight narrowing of the eyes, she said on a rising note, in an aggressive sing-song: "You're looking for your father, aren't you? You won't find him here, you know! Oh no, you won't find him here."

"Where is he, then?" Hugo asked, knowing that when he heard the answer he would feel a fool for having asked.

"He's up at Old Coldmouth graveyard, that's where he is. And a lot you care!"

Hugo, with no answer to that, asked: "And who are you?"

"I'm Miss Graley. I was his housekeeper. I looked after him well before he died and he left me everything. It's no good you trying to do anything about it. Your father made special mention of you in his will, how you'd gone off like that and taken your mother and he'd never heard a word

84

from you. He said you weren't to have a thing. If it hadn't been for me he'd have died in the infirmary."

"I see."

"I've been waiting for you, Mr. Hugo. I knew you'd turn up sooner or later, and I said to myself when he turns up as like as not he'll try and make a lot out of it, so I'm telling you here and now there was nothing going on. I'm a decent woman. There was nothing like that."

Hugo said: "I came to see my father, nothing more. I'll go now," he brushed past her, eager to get away, but in the hall, where the walls were still coated with paint like green glue, he stopped and said: "You can have the other stuff, but I'd be glad to have the model frigate in the front room."

With indignant emphasis, she replied: "Your father said you were to have nothing. *Nothing*."

Hugo left the house, jerking the door to behind him, then, as he had done a thousand times before, putting his hand against it to prevent the slam that made his father rage. Walking up the street, it occurred to him that had he tried persuasion he would have got the ship. She had not said 'No'; it was he that had taken her answer for 'No'. Though for years he had forgotten the model's existence, now, having failed to get it, he felt deprived and angry. He could not immediately bring himself to leave the neighbourhood of his loss. In the distance he saw the light of the public-house and he wandered along to it, slowly, with the belief that in a moment the woman would pursue him and hand the frigate to him. When he reached the corner he looked back, but no door had opened behind him. He stood a while, absurdly hopeful still, and watched the house disappearing into the black chill of night. It remained shut.

85

He entered the public bar. It was small, gloomy and sour-smelling. The few customers had the look of having grown old there. The face of the barman had that ghostly familiarity Hugo had seen on other faces about the city.

The barman stared at Hugo and at last said: "Mr. Fletcher's boy, isn't it?"

"Yes."

"Thought so. Knew your father well."

"Did he come here?" Hugo hoped by equalling the other's warmth to ward off whatever disapproval his father had roused against him; but there was no sign of disapproval. Perhaps, after all, his father had told them nothing.

The barman leant across the bar and spoke to those on the other side: "You remember Mr. Fletcher!" he told them.

There was a murmur or two of agreement, no great enthusiasm.

"Thin gent," pursued the barman, "iron-grey hair, wore glasses. Always in here, he was. Died about 1944, wasn't it?" He looked at Hugo.

Hugo nodded, not knowing.

"And your mum? What's she up to these days?"

"Dead, too. She was killed in one of the early raids."

"Oh! Sorry to hear that." The man looked glum a moment, then sprang back to his natural humour. "I'll never forget," he told his small, dim audience, "how Mr. Fletcher used to tell that story about the scissors. Oh, quite a character, he was."

"Was he?" Hugo was too surprised to disguise surprise. "And what was the story about the scissors?"

"You know it! 'Knife,' I said: 'Scissors,' said she?"

Hugo, amazed at the thought of his father telling that or any story, shook his head, realising too late that the man, supposing he did not know it, was preparing to tell it.

"It's about an obstinate woman, see? And he'd say: 'And there we were out in the punt and I said to her: "Did you see that bloke cutting that painter with a knife?" "I see'd him cut it with scissors," says she . . .' " The barman, as he spoke, looked round at his customers, who sat with the remote smiles of those too polite to say they have heard it all before.

" '. . . and then she comes up a second time: "Knife," says I: "Scissors," says she, just able to gasp it out: and down she goes again. The third time she comes up: "Knife," says I; and she opens her mouth but can't say a word, but I'm blowed if she don't lift her hand and go like this in the air.' "

The laughter came weakly upon his riotous finish. To regain ground he added quickly: "He was a one, your father. After he'd had a few beers we'd always get him to tell that story; and he'd tell it, his face as straight as a judge. He didn't smile much. Smiling gave him a funny look."

"Atrophied muscle," said a small man who, hands spread on knees, sat rigid, gazing at an empty glass.

"Was that what it was?" the barman murmured and, as though the whole subject had suddenly ceased to interest him, he turned his back and started washing glasses.

Hugo took this opportunity to retreat to the darkest end of the bar and this was rightly taken by the others as a sign that he wished to be regarded as out of sight. Standing there, he wondered what had brought his father to this place. When Hugo was a child, Mr. Fletcher had been a man who disapproved of public-houses. Was it under Miss Graley's influence he had so mellowed he could come here often, and tell a funny story?

Hugo could scarcely believe it. Yet, as he grew up, he had realised his father was human enough. The smile that had so frightened him as a child had been as physical as a limp. The accusations with which his father had tormented his family were, in fact, self-accusations. And his mother with her: "Why is he so cruel to me?", her "What have I done to deserve this?", her "He called me a fat fool! He says I've ruined his life!"—she, with all that injury to her credit, was, nevertheless, a fool.

In early days, when her husband was on active service, their relationship had been, at worst, an irritant. Mrs. Fletcher did not let it worry her. She was a jolly woman and to Hugo her laughter had seemed the most delicious in the world. It was in the confinements of Henley Street that the marriage had become a martyrdom.

There were intervals of peace when Mr. Fletcher was painting something, but when he wandered unemployed about the house he exuded malignancy—or so it seemed to his wife and son. When Mrs. Fletcher asked for her house-keeping allowance, he would snarl contempt at her extravagance and let her wait an hour or two before throwing the money on the table. Could she have shown spirit, she would soon have got the better of him, but she was easily intimidated. She, who used to find life an unceasing entertainment, became afraid to laugh at all. If she heard her husband enter, she would break off abruptly and take on an expression of nervous guilt that Hugo found unbearable. When he, outgrowing his own fear, saw hers as ridiculous, he would urge her: "Don't be frightened. He won't hurt you. He doesn't mean what he says," but Mrs. Fletcher was not to be persuaded out of her fear. She enjoyed it. Yes, he had come to realise that. She found satisfaction in self-pity.

Yet, impatient though he became of her and the hollow note in her laughter, he always saw as serious and binding his promise to take her away. It was a promise that had to be kept.

The barman glanced over his shoulder and, seeing Hugo standing there alone, beer undrunk, he moved down to him and said confidentially: "I was sorry to hear that about your mum. Hope I haven't brought it all back, like?"

Hugo, collecting himself quickly, shook his head, producing an effect of restrained emotion, so the man, to give him time, said tactfully:

"A nice little body. Of course she never came here. I never really knew her, but we saw her about. We all liked her."

In the obituary pause that followed, Hugo reflected how small a circle that 'all' covered. A gay woman, a pleasure-loving woman, encased in dullness by a husband as ponderous as a grave-stone! Hugo swallowed down his drink, said his 'Good-nights' and made his way back to the harbour by a maze of back street he could have covered blind-folded.

To save money and expend time, Hugo returned to Ridley on foot. There were two routes: the longer by the promenade, the other through the bombed area across which the wind raged unchecked. Hugo chose the bombed area, and in the midst of it paused and looked about him, wondering where was the shelter in which his mother had been killed.

The shelter had received a direct hit. Finding everyone dead inside, the authorities had sealed it up. The dead had been given no other tomb. Mrs. Fletcher's identity disc was one of those found among the confusion of blood and limbs, so Hugo, listed as her next-of-kin, had been told of her death. The letter described the shelter as situated in East Coldmouth: no more than that.

As he gazed around, half expecting to see some sign or memorial, he suddenly stopped, then turned abruptly and took the side street to the promenade. He would not look for her grave. The past had been rejected and she with it. Nothing remained here that could renew its hold upon him.

Days passed at Ridley House and no one spoke to Hugo. Outside the house there was no one to whom he could speak. Indeed, except for Tilly, he had forgotten even the names of his old acquaintances. As for Tilly—that visit must wait. He had neither plan with which to approach her or will to conceive one. Now he even hesitated to walk along the cliff-top in case he came upon her.

He took his exercise on the promenade. He joined the Free Library in the Ridley High Street and started reading his way through the detective novels, each of which was much like the others in shape, colour and content. They were books frequently borrowed, shabby and smelling of old clothes. Many of them he had read before in Egypt but usually he did not realise this until he was well into the plot.

Books that were more than entertainment he had stopped reading after he had taken his scholarship to St. Aubyn's. There he wanted only to ally himself with the great—the rugger boys, the boys from comfortable homes, the boys with family businesses like bastions behind them. They did not need to study, much less read for reading's sake.

Now, lying on his bed at Ridley, having no habit of concentration and his eyes growing tired of the page, he would be assailed by a sense of the inanity of a book and, putting it down, would sink into a stupor of boredom which left only his hearing awake.

Gradually, without knowing the geography of the house, its noises came to have meaning for him. There was a bathroom at the end of the passage used by Hugo and the Martyns. Someone—Kyra Martyn, he might have guessed—bathed there at the most unlikely hours of day and evening. (Hugo himself bathed at seven in the morning, when, the boiler being low, the water was luke-warm.) Hugo could hear the rush of the bath filling, the doors opening and shutting, the quickly-pouring hot tap turned off and the slower cold tap turned on, then the long silence while Kyra lay in the water, and he imagined her thin-bodied, sallow-skinned, not desirable.

He had never seen the kitchen, but he came to recognise the long hiss and thump in the pipes that resulted from turning on one of the kitchen taps. In the hall there was a visitor's cloak-room with a large, mahogany-seated water-closet that was flushed by pulling up a brass handle. When it was pulled there would come from somewhere under Hugo's bedroom floor a great gulping and stamping of water that went on for fifteen minutes.

The footsteps of Mrs. Martyn and Mrs. Prosser were, he learnt, very different. Martyn's, of course, were unmistakable. When he heard a fourth set of steps in the passage, he jumped up and looked out of the door and saw an old woman with pink-ringed eyes, placing her bucket and knee-pad before settling down to scrub the floor. Hugo would have been glad to talk to her could he have thought of anything to say, but, as it was, he met her blank stare blankly and shut the door again.

The first grey and gusty weeks of September were followed by a period of delicate warmth: a delicious, unexpected gift of warm weather just when it seemed summer had ended. As one day followed another without change, it was as though a new season, cooler than summer, milder than autumn, had settled upon the earth. It reminded Hugo of the few winter weeks in Upper Egypt when the air touched the lips with a scent and sweetness like nectarines; and he was suddenly reconciled with his native climate that could produce such surprises.

Becoming pleased with life, he wished there was someone to whom he could say of the weather "How beautiful!" and meet, if nothing more, agreement. Most of all he wished he might speak to Martyn again, and again experience the sense of his sympathy from which he was now cut off. In spite of all his nature's precautions against rebuff, he tried at meal-times to catch Martyn's eye, but the headmaster never looked in his direction.

Hugo took breakfast, luncheon and supper at the table. At tea-time, if he were in, Mrs. Prosser would bring upstairs a cup of tea, which she left on a tray outside his room. One afternoon, when he had drunk his tea and was bleak with boredom at the coming empty evening, he looked from the window and saw Charles Martyn cross the lawn and disappear into the trees that, grown ragged and yellow during the weeks of wind, were now aglow like the heart of a fire. Hugo felt an impulse to follow him that was as compelling as inspiration. He was convinced if they met out of sight of the house he would be able to speak.

A moment later he was crossing the lawn and rehearsing his speech. He murmured with emotion, a little drunkenly: "I did not really blame you. Even when I was bawling at you like a fool, I knew you were not to blame."

When he reached the spinney, he saw Martyn climbing the chalk path to the top of the downs. Hugo had planned for them to meet in the lap of the cliff-top. Now he stopped, allowing Martyn to get ahead, and sat on the seat where he had sat on the night of his arrival, and felt about him the softness of his native climate which then had seemed so alien and harsh. He could see the house through the thinning trees. In this mist- and fire-tinged light, the bricks glowed a rich and unearthly pink, while the green of the lawn, softened by a bloom of damp, seemed fluid, its colour as much silver as green.

Something creaked in the air above him. He looked up and saw, in a sky milky but dusted with gold as with a gilding powder, a pair of geese leisurely passing and stretching their necks as though to sip at the delicious air.

All seemed to him omens of reconciliation. He had to hold himself from running after Martyn. He must not catch him up too soon. Although he had no cause to think it, he was certain that were Kyra or Mrs. Prosser to over look their meeting, they would destroy it.

At last he felt it safe to go.

When he reached the top of the cliff he could see the white flank of the Webleys' house with its evergreens folded about it like dark wool. The white wall was touched by the sunset so that it seemed translucent, a wall of golden glass. He looked away from it at once, not wishing to consider it at that moment, and saw the sea still and powdery as a gauze. Over the crest the path dropped a little and Hugo saw Martyn again.

The headmaster was moving slowly, but suddenly he started stepping out with such animation of purpose that Hugo looked about to see his goal. There was another person on the cliff-top, a woman seated with a red coat spread beneath her.

Hugo came to a standstill. His first thought was that the woman might be Tilly; but, of course, it was not Tilly. This was a very young woman, a girl. Martyn strode directly towards her, but when he neared her he hovered uncertainly and seemed to hesitate before speaking. So they had not met before! He bent towards her in an attitude of apology. She looked up and her laugh came to Hugo on the still air small and high as the cry of a bird. Hugo watched enviously while Martyn talked: then the girl moved her hand that was resting on the coat and Martyn sat down beside her.

"And that's that!" said Hugo to himself, his whole mood fallen. It was as though he had lost both Martyn and the girl. After all, he might have seen her first and approached her; yet he knew he would scarcely have noticed her at all.

Now, what was he to do? He did not know. He did not
want to go on. Even though, facing the sea as they were,
they would probably not have seen him, he hesitated to pass
them. Besides, he did not want to approach the Webleys'
house. Had he not been led by Martyn, he would not have
come up here at all.

He turned to the house before he went and gave it a long
look. That secure home! Had he grown up there, what
might life not have given him?

As he walked back to the school, aimless and disappointed,
his thoughts turned against Martyn. 'The old lecher!' he
thought, 'picking up women! A young girl, a kid, a mere
kid! Really, he's just an old idiot! An idiot who let his
son swindle him.' His thoughts ran on: 'And he's a snob!
He's determined to keep me at arm's length. He may have
swindled me, but I did worse—I didn't accept it like a
"gent"!' Growing angry, he told himself he had been
ridiculous to imagine there might be any point of contact
between him and Martyn. And what did he care, anyway?

Approaching Ridley again, he wondered what to do.
There was so little money left in his account, he had decided
to draw out no more than five pounds a fortnight; but
inactivity was expensive. When he went into Coldmouth,
he was tempted to spend for the sheer occupation of spending. Now, without the price of a pint of beer in his pocket,
he wandered into the school, wishing, above all things,
he were safely back in Menteh. There he had had his salary
and nothing on which to spend it but rent, food and arak.
His friends had been ready-made for him and, as friends
were, he supposed, as good as any others.

He reached his room. Throwing himself on his bed he

gave himself up to a nostalgic contemplation of his Egyptian life; a life he had despised while he saw no escape from it. He had lived in one of a block of six modern flats built by a Cairo speculator. The block looked impressive enough, but bedding and mats hung from the windows all day long, and the entrance hall was cluttered with refuse which it was no one's business to clear away. He had been a member of a government service called the Public Instruction that employed hundreds of nondescript young Englishmen like himself. He had heard of it first when a pupil-teacher in Coldmouth; he had recognised it at once as one of those bolt-holes kept in sight by young men who live monotonous lives. It had seemed to him more possible or practicable than either the Foreign Legion or the fabled trip round the Horn in a tramp steamer. For one thing, he had actually known the brother of a man employed by the P.I. in the Delta. The brother was a fellow-student at the Teachers Training College, and he was always ready to talk about the P.I.—"Where we'll all end up. You see if we don't!" It was a joke service. There was the standard story about the young man who wrote home: 'Please don't tell my mother I've joined the P.I. She thinks I play a piano in a brothel.' And another about the teacher in a village near Wadi Halfa who, during the summer, sat before his class with a dozen tins of beer on his desk and a chamber-pot beneath it.

In a time of little money and few jobs, they had all kept the P.I. in sight, but only Hugo had fled to it. His time there had been neither happy nor unhappy. Like his war years in the Army, it had been an interval of expectancy. Now it seemed to him one could spend one's whole life in expectancy and lose nothing.

During his leave he would go to Cairo or Alexandria, stopping at cheap *pensions* and finding himself a Levantine girl-friend. When term-time started he would return to Menteh without regret. There one day passed much like another, and as each ended in the delicate colours of evening, he would find one or other of his friends ready to gossip in Abdul's garden. The virtue of this life was that nothing was demanded of him. He kept himself in reserve like a fighting man for whom a call might come. The only slight disturbance of his tranquillity came from Abdul's tendency to behave as though a special understanding placed him and Hugo together and apart from the others. Hugo, for instance, had been the only one to meet Abdul's wife.

The occasion was treated by Abdul as one of special honour to Hugo. An invitation to tea was issued several days ahead and Hugo was received, not in the garden, but in the house.

"Enter the salon," said Abdul in the most formal manner. "Everything that I have is yours."

The salon contained a large dining-table, a French gilt sofa and fifteen gilt chairs set side by side round the walls. There was nothing else in Menteh to equal this ostentation. Madame Fatteh, of course, did not wish to appear until the men had eaten. It had been an agonising meal for Hugo, who always found Abdul alone a bore. Hugo did not take sugar in his tea. Abdul refused to believe this. Hugo, he was sure, was politely belittling himself by refusing sugar, so, in homage to such modesty, Abdul put three lumps in his cup. Hugo shut his eyes and gulped down the tea while his host smiled beneficently. To the second cup, not to be refused, four lumps were added to confirm the compliment.

When this was drunk Abdul excused himself and left the room.

Ten minutes later the sound of Abdul's earnest persuasion and a stifled giggling came from behind the door. At last, with an air of dramatic dignity, Madame Fatteh made her entry. She was a large, faded woman of thirty in a black dress. She was not veiled—Abdul was too advanced to permit such a thing—but she held a black chiffon scarf as though always about to cover her face. She could not maintain the dignity of her entry for long. Like someone playing a part in a charade, she stitched her mouth in to hide her laughter, and as Hugo, responding ceremoniously, rose, kissed her hand and said how greatly he appreciated the honour of this meeting, she collapsed into giggles, and at each word giggled the more helplessly until tears filled her eyes and Abdul sternly ushered her out.

A few minutes passed, then he returned to the tea-things, his smile breaking through his frown as though he had just admonished, but not seriously, an adored child. Hugo paid him the usual compliments. Abdul pressed Hugo to more of the sugary, untidy-looking cakes and urged him to drink a third cup of tea. As though the privilege accorded Hugo had now bound him to Abdul for ever, Abdul said they were as brothers and could reveal their hearts to one another. Hugo imagined he knew all about Abdul's heart.

The meeting with Madame Fatteh being over, Hugo felt acutely bored. The crowded, stuffy room, the afternoon heat, the flies dragging their sticky feet over the sticky cakes, the taste of sweet tea in his mouth and Abdul's talk about the beauties of friendship—all, all oppressed him so that he almost nodded with sleep. Suddenly, finding the situation unbearable, he had clutched his head, looked at his watch and shouted: "Good God! I must go. At once, at once. An important date."

"What? Where?" Abdul's face, alarmed, agonised, stared too close to him. He jumped to his feet and went in a confusion of apologies and good-byes, giving no explanation and knowing Abdul must know there was none he could give.

Later he was annoyed with himself, certain his behaviour in this small community must lead to strained relations with Abdul; but it did not. Abdul, apparently, had invented his excuses for him, and when the four of them were together would catch his glance and smile as though he and Hugo met on a different plane, in a peculiar bond of sympathy. Hugo, for safety's sake, would smile back, but he was discomforted as though being signalled to in a language he did not understand.

If Abdul, like a schoolboy, wanted a 'special friend'— well, that was understandable enough! But Abdul's complacent belief that he and Hugo were set apart from the others irritated Hugo, not because he was fond of Aston and Père Legouis, but because he was not more fond of Abdul. All three exasperated him equally at times, and equally gave him essential companionship. There was nothing each did not know about the others—yet he had broken away from the group as though it comprised the chance acquaintances of a day. Remembering them now, he remembered them with a sentiment that was no more than indulgence of a mood. He knew that, could he return there, he would exist again in the hope of leaving them, and leave them as willingly and casually as before.

Having come to an end of these memories and grown restless again, he jumped up from his bed. The house seemed empty. Moving like a trespasser, he went to Classroom A. For some reason, after his fit of anger, he had forgotten all about the drawing on the blackboard. Now he went to look at it. The blinds darkened the room. He switched on the light just long enough to see that the board had been cleaned. With a slight sense of triumph, he made his way downstairs and began to explore the passages that branched to right and left of the hall.

The first room he opened was the kitchen, large, old-fashioned, dark and not over-clean. Some fresh herrings lay in a strainer, their silver catching the last light beneath the window. 'Supper,' thought Hugo without enthusiasm, for in Egypt food, if nothing else, had been rich and plentiful.

The door opposite the kitchen was marked 'Common Room', and he looked in on the heavy brown lincrusta of what had once been a dining-room and now, with its cheap tables and chairs, had been worn to the bone by a crowd of small boys.

He crossed to the other passage. The door at the end opened on to the study in which Hugo had had his talk with Martyn. The door to the right was marked 'Masters' Common Room'. There, surely, he had some rights. He entered. It was the twin of the dining-room, but the walls had been painted white. There were five worn, leather armchairs and a couple of writing-desks. Round the walls were illustrated the careers of Hogarth's 'Idle and Industrious Apprentices'. The grate was filled by a large, old-fashioned gas-fire. On one side of the chimney-breast were fitted three shelves, all empty. A label was stuck on each. Hugo crossed and read the names:

BERNARD GLASS
J. F. STEBBING
M. MAURICE

Had Maurice been a French teacher? Did the M. stand for Monsieur? Glass he pictured as a young man, thick-haired, fair, with the heavy good looks that go with a coarse skin—genial, yes, genial; and of leftist views. A man who might holiday with a ruck-sack, or go climbing—rock climbing, that was it. Perhaps he was one of those who climbed with ropes on newly-tried faces in Wales and Scotland. And longed to go to the Himalayas.

Stebbing was, of course, an older man, a sober-sided fellow, informed but not informing. And a bachelor. Perhaps Glass ragged him a little and Stebbing took it well. "All right, Glass, my dear fellow, you're young yet. When you're my age . . ." or "Now, Glass, you take it from one who knows . . ."

And Maurice? Hugo could get so little response from that name, he looked about him as though the room held three companions, Glass, Stebbing and Maurice.

In the twilight there was only emptiness.

At that moment, oddly, the memory of Abdul returned to his mind and he thought: 'Why the devil should I have been bothered by him?'

He was about to switch on a reading-lamp when he saw a brilliant star of light in a corner by the book-case. There was a hole in the wall. The light must come from Martyn's room. Hugo put an eye to the hole and the corner of a red coat flickered out of view. He was astounded. Martyn had brought the girl in. And how had they got there without coming through the house? Was it possible they had been there in the semi-darkness all the time?

No, for the girl said in the tone of a new arrival: "I can only stay a tick."

Martyn replied urgently: "Do stay a little while. I'm all alone here."

The girl laughed, but her laugh was not so pleasant as it had been in the open air. "I don't know that I should, you being all alone." Her tone was a provocation but Martyn seemed unaware of that. His manner was no more than friendly; he said:

"It is very good of you to come and keep me company."

She laughed again at that. She was moving about the room. As she walked away from Hugo, her voice grew indistinct; then, returning, she said:

"Who are these old dears?"

"My grandparents," Martyn answered.

Hugo missed her comment. He gave up trying to see into the room. Pressing his ear to the hole, he heard more clearly:

"And who's this?"

"My first wife."

"Oh!" A pause, then without enthusiasm: "Nice face, isn't it? Doesn't the other one mind?"

"My keeping this photograph? Why should she? Can one feel jealous of the dead?"

"I don't know, I'm sure." The girl spoke flatly, no doubt wanting to leave the profitless subject of Martyn's wives, but Martyn now pursued it, so that Hugh wondered if it were simply to hear of it that the girl had been brought here.

"She was called Patricia. She was exactly the same age as I was. I sometimes feel if she had lived I would have never grown old. That's ridiculous, I know. But Kyra, that's my present wife, makes me feel older than I am. Of course, she used to live a different sort of life. She was an actress. She knew brilliant people. Perhaps that's why she seems to have elbowed me right into the 'old fogey' class and slammed the door on me.

"Poor you!" the girl said earnestly. "Perhaps it's just she doesn't understand you."

Martyn, again unconscious of this conventional feint, was absorbed in his own subject: "Patricia and I lived in London, in Pimlico . . ."

"Pimlico!" The girl was surprised. "I saw a film about Pimlico. Not what you'd call a classy part, is it?"

"We liked it. Our house faced the river." Martyn, it seemed, was moving about, so Hugo could catch only an occasional sentence. "She painted in water-colours . . . the grey river, the fog, the wet, yellow-streaked sunsets. . . . We could walk to the Poetry Bookshop . . ."

When a pause came, the girl politely asked: "What happened to her?"

"She died . . ." Martyn must have swung down to the end of the room here, for Hugo could not catch a word until he passed the seated girl, saying: "A party in Chelsea. . . . A beautiful night, so we walked back . . ." his words were lost again, then Hugo heard: "I went into the sitting-room and she was in a chair, lying over the arm, one hand touching the floor . . . a long mauve dress embroidered with beads. . . . We had only been married three years. Brian was a year old when she died."

103

"Very sad," said the girl with a sigh of boredom. "You never know with a weak heart, do you?"

"When I was last in London," said Martyn, standing still, "I had a look at the house. I liked it just as much. It is like a country house, with a french window opening on to the front garden. There was a winter jasmine breaking into flower. I think it was the very one I planted. The river was the same—the yellow sunset, just the same: while she, who had once seen it and put it all so beautifully on to paper, has no more sight or consciousness than the dust."

There was a pause; then, the recital having come to an end, the girl said cheerfully: "Very sad indeed. But what I always say is, grieving won't bring them back. All this must have happened a long time ago."

"Yes, twenty-five years ago. Quarter of a century."

"There you are, you see."

Someone coughed slightly—not in the next room, but in the room where Hugo stood. He jerked himself upright, growing nervously cold, and in the last pewter bleakness of the dusk he saw Kyra Martyn standing, watching him. Hugo looked away, his cheeks growing red, shocked not only for his eavesdropping but for Martyn.

She said: "So you've discovered the peep-show?"

"What . . .?" began Hugo.

"The hole in the wall. I should like to know who made it. I always suspected the maths. master, Stebbing. He was capable of anything. Anyhow, there it is! And I suppose you've been hearing all about poor Patricia in her mauve dress? And those wishy-washy water-colours?"

Hugo did not know what to say. "I heard something," he said and looked at Kyra, who, her chin raised, her expression contemptuous, seemed, in this lack of light, the girl who had stood high on the stage between the double windows. He thought: 'She is still the most beautiful woman I have ever seen.'

"Well"—she made a movement with her hand, an actress's movement—"I hope it amused you as much as it amused me." She turned effectively and left him alone.

He remained still, feeling as though he had had a narrow escape. He had not realised before how much Kyra unnerved him. His hands, pressed into his pockets, were hot and damp. Really, it was as though he had expected her to devour him! He wondered what effect the sound of her voice—and it was a voice that carried far—could have had on Martyn and the girl. The light had gone out. He pressed his ear to the hole again. There was a long silence—then he heard the squeak of the window cautiously raised; a scrape of feet as the girl climbed out. A slower and more difficult scramble as Martyn followed.

When Hugo stood up again there was darkness and silence everywhere. He felt about him an emptiness as abysmal as death.

He thought of Kyra. Had her departure had something of an invitation about it? Would he find her in the sitting-room? With a mounting hope and excitement, he followed after her—but outside there was only darkness. The sitting-room door was ajar and darkness was within. He went along to the hall and saw beneath the kitchen door a thread of light. He crossed to it and threw it open. Only Mrs. Prosser was inside. She had a knife in her hand and was at the table gutting the herrings. She turned and, seeing him, she grinned.

"Hello, dearie! Lonely? Why not come in for a chat?"

He looked at her as he had once looked at his unwanted ally Vernon, then, shaking his head, he closed the door on the sight of her and went to his room.

CHAPTER IV

NOW that both Kyra and Mrs. Prosser had spoken to him, it seemed a rift had come into the tension that held them all in silence. At luncheon next day the two women began to speak of household matters, and when these were concluded Mrs. Prosser, with a look at Kyra which told Hugo this was a game they had played before, turned to Martyn and assumed the face of ill-tidings. She said:

"I think I ought to tell you, sir, that kitchen wall doesn't look too good to me."

Martyn started. His usually mild expression changed to anxious annoyance. He looked at Mrs. Prosser as though any fault in any wall must be of her making, and asked discouragingly: "Which wall, Mrs. Prosser?"

"Why, the outside wall, of course. It's that damp, I think it's dangerous. My brother was in the building trade, as you know, and he often said to me: 'With these old properties, you never know,' and this is one of the worst *I've* seen. He said: 'Neglect a damp wall and anything might happen.' "

"Well, what could happen?" asked Martyn with a weary show of fight.

"Creeping damp can set in. A very nasty thing that is, and no cure for it. Except you could get a new damp-proof course—but what would that cost? A thousand pounds, I

reckon. Or you could get wet rot into the woodwork."
She lifted her chin and after a pregnant pause added darkly:
"Or *worse*."

"Worse!" Martyn now looked a man harassed beyond
bearing. "What do you mean by worse?"

Mrs. Prosser replied in a tone so sombre the words seemed
muffled: "Dry rot."

"Good God, surely not!"

Martyn's agonised reaction made even Mrs. Prosser
seem to pity him. She relented somewhat. "I don't say
you've got it, mind you. It's just that in a damp place like
this it'ud be a miracle if you hadn't. All I can say is, keep a
sharp look-out. Take the floorboards up every now and
then. If you don't, well . . ."

"But is dry rot caused by damp?" Martyn gazed at her in
the misery of his ignorance.

"Certainly it is," she replied severely. "What else would
cause it?"

"Dryness, I should have thought." He spoke with a
touch of sad humour which caused Kyra to make a comment:

"Don't be silly, Charles."

Here Martyn showed a little spirit. "The last time, when
Mrs. Prosser suspected dry rot under the Common Room
floor, she said it was caused by lack of ventilation."

"That's one of the causes," said Mrs. Prosser. "Now, my
brother . . ."

Martyn interrupted with a sigh: "Perhaps your brother
would like to come here and give us his opinion."

"But I've told you before, sir, my brother's gone to
Australia."

"So he has. So he has. Lucky fellow!"

"Do you think you would be happier in Australia?" Kyra asked, coldly.

"Perhaps not. But at least I wouldn't be worrying about damp."

"Oh, you'd find something else to worry about. You're always in a state of incipient panic about this wretched house. Let it fall down. Who cares? I've always hated the place. Only a fool would have taken it. Haven't you enough to occupy your mind this quarter with the rates and water rates coming in, as well as ground rent, schedule A, electricity, gas and telephone?"

Martyn, staring before him, said: "I don't know where the money's coming from."

"We will have to take in lodgers," said Kyra, her face expressing nothing.

Whether she meant this seriously or not, Martyn answered seriously: "Our lease does not permit us to sub-let."

At this Kyra leant back and gave a shriek of laughter, while Mrs. Prosser twisted her face into the comical wryness of a clown, then, turning and meeting Hugo's watching eyes, she gave him a wink as broad as the wink of a panto-mime horse. After this she started to pursue her success:

"*And* I should have mentioned the roof up in the attics. There's a good few leaks need doing before the winter proper. The roof *is* your responsibility, isn't it?"

"Everything's my responsibility," replied Martyn.

"Yes. I was just saying to Miss Kyra yesterday, I was saying *what* a pity you bought that lease. And I expect you'll have to fork out a pretty penny to do the place up at the end of it all."

"We'll worry about that when the time comes," said

Martyn dryly, and, it being obvious that his emotions on this subject were, for the moment, exhausted, Mrs. Prosser said no more.

Hugo left the table with annoyance at the women and their baiting of Martyn, but he felt a new dimension of grievance as he reflected that it was Martyn who had advertised for an investor in this ramshackle place. The fact that he had already lost everything did not mitigate the later discovery that his investment would in any case have been a poor bargain. He was convinced again that Martyn really was a rogue and confirmed in his intention to stay at Ridley, a burden upon the lot of them and a figure of reproach.

That evening, that loomed the more oppressive for being a Saturday, a holiday evening, he decided he must go out. He would spend what money he had while he had it.

Kyra, at luncheon, had mentioned to Mrs. Prosser that she would not be in for supper. Hugo listened for her departure in the late afternoon. When he heard her usual bang of the front door, he felt a need to hurry after her. The hallway was growing dark, and he had reached the stairs before he noticed Martyn standing below in the hall watching the front door that had closed behind Kyra.

Martyn was so transformed by his alertness that, for the first time, he looked to Hugo a man capable of happiness. He stood for half a minute or so, a black trilby hat in his hand, then, certain that Kyra was well out of the way, he dodged back to leave the house by the back door. Hugo wondered: "What is he up to?" But what did it matter, anyway.

By the time Hugo was able to leave the house, Kyra was out of sight. He could see in the distance the bus making its return journey to Coldmouth, and he knew she would be on it. Without reason, he felt disappointed, knowing that even could he have followed on her heels, she would have had little time to waste on him.

It was stormy outside. The fine weather had gone in a night. A grey, wet-swollen sky hung over the belt of evergreens. The giant lime tree by the gate was stripped almost bare. As Hugo crossed the garden a concourse of leaves, of a pure golden yellow, was swept up by the wind and spiralled about him, then fell to trickle and tinkle along the flagged paths. Behind the distant dockyard cranes there was a cold sunset: the misty air had a damp and melancholy smell.

Filled with a sense of time lost and time passing here in nothingness, Hugo set out for the promenade as though his life's purpose were in his going. A bus arrived at the tarmac terminus as he passed through the school gates. Afraid of missing it, he sped across the field and swung himself breathlessly on board: then sat for ten minutes in the front seat, consumed by irritation that the bus did not start and take him—where? Nowhere. And because there was nowhere to go, he felt the more impatient.

The driver and conductor were smoking at the sea rail, watching the sun slide down into the sea. Hugo kept his gaze on them, willing them to get started; and, at last, with maddening leisureliness, they took their places and the bus set out.

The roofs of Coldmouth cut off the last gleam of the sun. Hugo felt that, wherever he was going, he was setting out too late. The bus seemed to be pressing forward away from the light into a heavy twilight. There would be no more fine weather. Ahead lay winter, with the gales flinging fans of spray across the promenade, and life retreated behind closed doors. There came back upon him, like a lasso from the past, the black gloom of those winters when, to escape his home, he would pretend to his mother he had somewhere to go and, without a penny in his pockets, spend the long hours walking in dark and rain.

"Those days are over," he said to himself, trying to throw off the memory—but were they over? For he would soon be penniless again. Soon, he realised, he would be forced to find some sort of job here, that he might have money to spend. However his presence and poverty and inactivity might affect Charles Martyn, he was beginning to fear that the chief sufferer was himself. He wondered what sort of job his qualifications and experience could bring him here. The best he might hope for would be a post in an elementary school—a post like the one he had held for a while, and hated, before he left England in 1939. Even were he willing to take such a post, there would be little chance of a vacancy before Christmas; and he should be doing something about it now.

The prospect depressed him, and when he left the bus at the Harbour Row, he went, as a gesture against the future, straight into the bar of the Drake Hotel. He regretted it at once. After all his years of spending only under necessity, he met in the glossy woodwork, the navy-blue bunker seats, the port-hole windows, the bell to be rung at closing time, the cloak-room doors marked 'Powder Room' and 'Officers' Mess', the decorations of whitewashed rope, all the intimidating indications of having to spend more than he could afford. It was called, of course, the 'Harbour Bar'. It sold no draught beer. He had to take lager, which he did not like, and he seemed to be the only one drinking that. Here, apparently, it was correct to order gin, or small emerald- or ruby-coloured drinks advertised as 'Bert the Barman's Specialities—Starboard and Port Lights'.

At once dazzled and derisive, Hugo carried his long, conspicuous lager glass over to one of the semi-circular blue seats set into recesses in the walls. He had taken one of his girls, a Greek, to a bar something like this in Alexandria, and her comment had been "God, how vulgar! and not even original." Had he had anyone to whom to say it, he would have been delighted to say: "God, how vulgar! and not even original," but, for all that, he was impressed as he would have been fifteen years before; for, somehow, the bar, being in Coldmouth, was another thing. Several minutes passed before he realised the voice of the woman in the next seat was that of Kyra Martyn. She had her back to Hugo and was sitting with a young man who, as Hugo swung round, met his eye and smiled. Hugo turned away quickly. Kyra glanced over her shoulder to see what had interested her companion, but did not turn far enough. Hugo was able to keep out of sight.

After this interruption she started to speak again in a tone of reiterated complaint: "But not to send a word . . . not a *word*, after getting safely away!" Then with a slight lift of tone: "Who would have thought he had it in him?"

"You seem pretty certain he *has* got away," the young man broke in.

Kyra answered sharply: "I can't imagine he'd either be such a fool as to stay—or, if he stayed, clever enough to remain uncaught." There was a longer pause before she added reflectively: "But I wouldn't have imagined he'd let Pippin down, either."

"He's let other people down. Why not Pippin?"

Kyra replied with the quiet of complete finality: "He was fond of Pippin. That's all."

Hugo, his head pressed against the curve of the wall behind his seat, his whole body intent on listening, held his breath in excitement that, at last, there was mention of Brian and his departure with the money, but he was not to hear more. The young man changed the subject:

"What are you all doing up there at Ridley?"

"Nothing. Just waiting."

"For what?"

Kyra's reply, if she made one, could not be heard. The long continued silence released Hugo from the strain of listening and he began to consider this person, Pippin, who seemed to have had some hand in the business. He emptied his glass and wondered if the situation justified the expense of refilling it. If, on his way from the bar, he could catch Kyra's eyes, might he not ask permission to join her and learn more? And if he dared do it, which would be the better approach—boldness or guileless friendliness? At last he jerked himself up and went to the bar; as he returned with his second glass he advanced on Kyra. She had recognised him, and now watched him with an irritated unwelcome.

He said: "May I join you?"

Her only reply was to nod at the seat opposite her. Hugo sat down beside her companion, the young man who had been lolling, watching Kyra with indifferent eyes, until Hugo approached. Now he sat up, his whole body taking on a self-conscious tautness, and lowered his eyelids and drew his mouth down in a smirk. When Hugo glanced at him he flickered open his eyes and slid them slowly round to give Hugo a look so openly inviting that Kyra turned her glance from one to the other of them, clearly wondering if the look had been justified.

"A case of mistaken identity." Hugo smiled at her.

She replied: "So I thought."

They both looked at the young man, who bridled a little and tutted with his tongue. Something about him had roused a sort of spite in Hugo, who would have been glad to hit out at anything that would relieve the sense of his life's frustration; but the sight of the young man folding like a dropped towel under his slap disturbed Hugo as though, having struck at something hard, he found it soft. The squabbles of maturity were not so straightforward as those of youth. They gave him none of the exhilaration he had known, in more triumphant days, after he had got the upper hand with the boys at Old Coldmouth.

Kyra introduced her companion as Kinky Bluett, but made no attempt to explain him. Almost at once she started the conversation on a course harmless to her: "Have you made any more discoveries at Ridley?"

"Do you mean have I been spying on your husband again?"

She shrugged slightly, looking as though his question had been an accusation. "Anyway," she said, "it all means nothing: all that mourning over his first wife. He got over it long ago. Now he's fingering an old wound, just to kid himself he can still feel something. It makes him a pretty fair bore. Poor Patricia, hanging over that chair, dead, her finger-tips trailing the floor." She crooked up one shoulder and dropped her hand from the seat in a sudden, appalling caricature of the dead—a lightning act that startled her audience; then she slumped back in her place smiling wryly. "Oh, dear, it took me a long time to get away from that woman. She cluttered my life up. I'm that most cluttered of creatures—a second wife."

Hugo, watching her, said nothing: she moved her hands nervously at her throat and went on from sheer need to keep the subject going: "When we first met—it was at a party shortly after I finished in *Message*—Charles said: 'I'm a great admirer of gifted women. My late wife was a very gifted painter,' and so on about Patricia every time we met until after we were married. Then I said: 'No more Patricia. She had her life; let me have mine.' "

"Can't say I blame you," said Kinky Bluett.

Kyra was about to speak again when she was distracted by the opening of the bar door. She raised her head, her lips parted, and said nothing until the new arrivals were in view; after which, relaxing, she turned and met Hugo's watchful stare.

The fact of her awareness of him, and her uncertainty of what he may have heard, began to give him a pleasing sense of being in control. He would leave her in uncertainty. He smiled across at her in what he hoped was an 'inscrutable' fashion, but her reaction swept his confidence from under him.

She said: "I'm interested to know what sent you beetling off to Upper Egypt—that's no place for a young man to choose. What were you running away from?"

He caught his breath, certain she had heard some gossip.

Mrs. Prosser must have got hold of something. When he did not reply, she rallied him, a certain malice in it all: "Let us hear your confession. What crime did you commit?"

Conscious of his own guiltlessness, he answered blankly: "No crime at all."

"What was the matter, then? Mother didn't love you enough? Oh, well, we all live off that old stockpot. No one ever loved me either, except perhaps . . ." before finishing that sentence, she caught herself up quickly with another: "Learn to enjoy your neurosis. Think how dull life would be without it."

He shook his head, smiling faintly and aloofly, hoping to retain his superior position. "I haven't got a neurosis."

"No? Just a nice normal boy? Then why Upper Egypt?"

"Why not?"

"I can think of a dozen reasons. But I asked you why you went."

Feeling she would force him some time to answer this question, he said: "I suppose someone has been gossiping about me? You've heard about the accident?"

"No. No one has said anything. Tell me about it."

He felt resentful now, as though he had been trapped into speaking—yet, what did it matter? They were bound to hear something sooner or later. He said: "I was driving a car that killed a girl. It was not my fault. There was a man in the car. He was drunk. He pulled the wheel round and we crashed into a crowd of people coming out of a cinema. Of course he didn't know what he was doing. I got the blame."

"Oh!" she spoke with her attention on a couple just entering the bar. She appeared not much interested in his story now she had heard it. "Must have shaken you. That poor girl!"

The girl? The girl, silly little fool, had been the least thing about it. All Hugo could remember of her was her father, an elderly, bearded man who, at the inquest, answered questions respectfully, saying 'sir' all the time, unaware, it seemed, of the tears coursing down his cheeks and into his beard. He apologised for his daughter, explaining that she had been the youngest of his seven children, so he had let her do much as she liked. He had said: "You see, sir, to the missis and me she was always our baby."

" 'Quids-in' was killed, too," Hugo said.

Kyra looked from the door and, not having heard what he said, gave him an encouraging smile: "Don't brood on it," she murmured from the great distance of her inattention.

The bar was filling up rapidly now with a Saturday night crowd. The door scarcely shut before it opened again, and Kyra watched it all the time. She seemed to him as remote as ever, but with a different remoteness. She was worn now, and her skin, in this harshly-lit, hot and smoky atmosphere, was damp and flushed, yet something remained of the beauty of the woman he had seen upon the stage. And it was as though she were still enclosed in the glass of the double window.

Kinky Bluett pushed at his arm and he had to look round. Smiling in a sulky way, Bluett asked: "Do you often come here?"

Hugo shook his head, not prepared to waste time on this young man. As soon as Kyra's glance returned to the table, Hugo, to get and hold her attention, spoke out boldly: "I could not help overhearing a few remarks you made before I joined you. Is it true that someone you know—someone called Pippin—expects to hear from your stepson, Brian?"

Well, he had succeeded! Kyra's eyes opened and she stared at him for several moments before she said, quietly:

"Naturally we all hope to hear from him. His father is terribly worried. He has disappeared. It would be funny if we didn't hope to hear from him."

"I didn't say 'hope'; I said 'expect'."

She went on looking at him as though he had said nothing pertinent. He was forced to explain further: "You gave me the impression that this person, Pippin, was . . ." he hesitated to make so bald a statement as 'an accomplice', instead he ended lamely: ". . . was rather 'in the know'."

Kyra shook her head as though uncertain of his meaning but certain it was based on misunderstanding. "No," she said innocently, "no one knows anything. As for hearing from Brian—it's not very likely we shall, is it? I mean, if he wrote saying: 'I'm in . . . in, say, the South of France,' we'd feel bound to inform the police, wouldn't we? and they would extradite him."

Hugo smiled in an exasperated way, knowing he would learn nothing. He said: "I'm glad you take so moral an attitude. And please forgive my interest in Brian's where-abouts. The money he went off with was all I had."

"Do you mean that?" she was surprised. "You invested all the money you had in that wretched school?"

"In your husband's school? Yes."

She grunted, then sniffed slightly. "Not much of an investment. You needn't feel too badly about Brian. It was just a question of whether you lost the money sooner or later."

119

"You mean I was cheated?"

"Not deliberately. On the contrary Charles believed that with your money and your help the place would soon be flourishing. He had the highest ideals, but he's the least effectual of men. He's . . ." she paused, then said abruptly: "Oh, he's hopeless."

"How did he come to take on Ridley House?"

"You may well ask. It was advertised in one of the Sunday papers. He saw the advertisement. It was all done behind my back. I was away in France, on a holiday, my first holiday abroad since the war. I came back to find he'd taken on that miserable house. Sunk all we had in it. A nice surprise for me. I could have murdered him."

Kinky Bluett gave a snigger of laughter, but Kyra looked as grim as she sounded.

Hugo said: "The house was empty for years. I often saw it when I was a child. The blinds were always down. I suppose it was in a pretty poor state?"

"Terrible. The Army had occupied it during the war. The War Office paid compensation on a 1945 estimate. That didn't mean much by the time we got it. The garden was a wilderness. Charles dug that up and planted it himself—but it was all too much for him."

"What about Brian?"

"Oh, Brian!" Her tone dismissed him. "The whole project was insane. In-*sane*! Yet. . . . Another man might have made a go of it. I don't know!" she sighed. "Charles isn't the sort to do well on his own. The whole project was doomed from the start." She looked into her glass as she spoke, then lifted a hand and somehow, with a gesture, conveyed to Hugo a situation of despairing failure.

She said: "When I first saw Ridley, I said to myself: 'This is a good place to get away from.' "

Suddenly she sat upright, got out her cigarettes, tapped one on the table and said: "Poor Charles!" with such contempt that Hugo felt angry. His own anger surprised him, for he had no reason to support Martyn against Kyra. Martyn had, in a manner, induced him into this situation, while Kyra was blameless—yet his instinct was for Martyn. To explain this he told himself he could not dismiss as contemptible the man with whom he had felt so completely in sympathy at their first meeting; that would be too much like dismissing himself.

Hugo wanted to say to Kyra: 'How did you come to marry Charles Martyn whom you despise so much? How did it happen that you, the actress in the *Message*, ended up as the wife of a provincial headmaster? What did you ever have in common?' but he did not know how to begin asking those questions. He might, he felt, have brought her to talk about herself if this idiotic boy, this Kinky Bluett, had not been seated imperturbably there, between them. He decided to keep to the subject of the school. He might, after a while, be able to get the details of the 'unfortunate friendship' which had given rise to gossip and the withdrawal of the grant. He said:

"But, after all, there was a school. It had got going. My solicitor was a pretty fair imbecile, but even he checked up that the place was on its feet. When did things start to go wrong?"

"They never went right. We began with twenty boys. We took them at cut prices to make a start. We ended with thirty. Only five of these ever paid the full fees, and we had three masters, Mrs. Prosser, a cook and a char, to say nothing of the upkeep of that mouldering old barn of a house. If you've been waiting around with some idea the school may get on its feet again, you're wasting your time. It never has been on its feet—except on paper."

"I'm waiting around because I have nowhere better to go."

"You must be pretty desperate."

"I am," he replied evenly. "It's too late to get another job this term. I'm not particularly well qualified and, with nothing to invest in another school, no one is going to jump at me. Jobs are not as plentiful as they were."

Kyra glanced uncomfortably at Kinky Bluett, but Kinky merely sat smiling, as aloof from the situation as Kyra herself had been when Hugo first heard of it. She said: "Even so, if I were in your place I should not care to hang around Ridley."

"What would you do?"

She gave him a glance, then looked down, seeming to retreat into a contemplative gloom while she moved her glass about, making a pattern of wet rings on the table top. Either she had no answer to his question or preferred not to give one. This, Hugo thought, was getting them nowhere. Then, noticing that her glass was empty, he supposed she was waiting for him to fill it.

"What are you drinking?" he asked.

Kinky replied without hesitation: "Gin," but dragged out the word so that it seemed reluctantly spoken.

Kyra said: "No. Why should you? This is on me." She drew a folded ten-shilling note from the depths of her bag and threw it over to Kinky.

"Certainly not." Hugo, scarcely knowing if he had enough to pay for them, crossed to the bar with an air and ordered two gins. His own glass, fortunately, was still half full. As he returned he found Kyra watching him with an amused curiosity and was suddenly elated, feeling her sharp-edged and rude, but not indifferent. Her quality was challenging. There was no doubt he was making an impression. He put the drinks down and, seating himself, was preparing to follow up a situation now, surely, in his favour, when her attention was again attracted to the door. This time her expression showed that the newcomer was the person for whom she had been watching. Hugo turned to see who it was. The man entering the bar was slight and small, with a delicate, pale face and a cloud of very fair hair. At first glance he looked like a youth of twenty, but as he approached his hair showed less gold than white, and his face was netted with fine lines. His youthful look dissolved until, as he paused beneath the central light, his face, corpse-pale and deeply hollowed, was the face of a man in late middle age. He glanced about him nervously.

Kyra, leaning from her seat, called quietly: "Pippin." Her voice carried, delicate and silver as a dart, through the uproar of the bar. He turned at once and, seeing her, smiled with vague tenderness like someone separated from reality by a narcotic.

"Pippin, come here." But he did not come. Lifting one hand in vague acknowledgment of her call, he began drifting round the bar as though carried by a wind.

"Pippin!" Her call was urgent and anxious, but his only response was to move to the door on the other side of the room and leave as though he heard nothing.

Kyra was pulling her coat frantically about her shoulders. She caught up her bag and gloves. "I must go after him."

"Shall I come with you?" Kinky asked.

"Yes, if you like." She went without a word to Hugo.

Kinky stood up, but before moving he emptied his glass, then, giving Hugo a slightly mocking smile, he followed her with leisurely rolling hips.

Hugo sat for some minutes supposing, so sudden and unexplained was their departure, that they would come back again. Kyra had not even touched her gin. Time passed. He realised they would not return. A chill descended on him; he felt slighted and alone. He might have stayed on to drink the gin, but he did not want it. He did not want to stay at all.

The bar was very crowded. People were pushing into any seats they could find. A large, barrel-chested young man with a wide moustache led over his pretty girl and said abruptly to Hugo: "Mind if we crowd in here?"

"I'm just going," Hugo said, and went.

Once out of the noise and brilliance of the bar, he was desolated by the emptiness of the street. He wished he had stayed inside. In winter the Harbour Row, with its public-houses, had the only life left to the town. The harbour waters, moving like black satin, were set here and there with lights, white, red and green. On a point near the station there was the sombre ultramarine bulb of a small Customs shed. To leave this area was to pass into outer darkness.

Hugo set out to walk to Ridley. Almost at once he was in the bombed waste-land where the wind sprang up like an enemy. An enemy! In Menteh, where one came so quickly to the town's edge, that abode of robbers, he would wander about alone, even out beyond the cultivation into the black reaches of the desert, with no fear of enmity. Enmity was for him an element of his native town. He did not expect to find it anywhere else. If it had existed in Menteh, he had not observed it.

But here, in Coldmouth, it was of the very nature of the place. He had discovered it early and grown up to anticipate it in every movement, to feel its slights in every word spoken. It had pursued him from Whittaker Road School to St. Aubyn's; and from St. Aubyn's to his life as a hanger-on of the boys he had known there.

The famous school had stood here. He stopped by the black abyss that held the moats and vaults of a medieval castle taken over by the school before the first war. It had been situated on the water-front beside the swimming-pool and had formed a bar between the harbour and the promenade. Bombed out of existence, it aroused no regrets in him.

As he wandered on he remembered the years he had spent in the cold stone classrooms. The last years had not been so bad, but the early ones had been the worst in his life. He had not been prepared for the sort of indifference he met there.

His mother, who must have guessed something of his miseries at Whittaker Road, had urged him to work for a scholarship. She assured him that at the Grammar School or St. Aubyn's he would meet 'nice' boys; would make friends of 'his own sort'; would 'feel at home'. He imagined he would find himself back in the comfortable, happy world he had inhabited before they moved to Old Coldmouth. The truth was he had felt less at home at St. Aubyn's than at

Whittaker Road. At Whittaker Road, after all, enmity had been attention, a sort of flattery. At St. Aubyn's he had simply been ignored. Being a poor boy among the sons of money-conscious tradespeople, he had been made to feel himself a nonentity. There was no reason why anyone should ever notice him; no reason unless he forced himself upon them.

To his elders he had seemed a senseless aggressor. They could not see against what he fought. To his contemporaries he was simply crazy. The result was that as he grew older and rose out of the anonymity of the lower forms, he earned a certain regard as one never to be trusted, amusing in some moods but always liable to bite. He recognised his position as that of an eccentric who need ask sympathy from no one. It was not a position on which time had much improved.

Halfway across the bombed area he stopped again. In his early childhood, in that irrecoverable period of happiness, they had lived here. Exactly here. Even in this chaos he could not forget the site of his grandfather's house—a red-brick Edwardian dormered house surrounded by a garden: not a beautiful house, but to him finer than any other in the world. Another doctor had lived in it after the Fletchers left. Hugo, when he cycled to and from the St. Aubyn's Playing Fields, would go out of his way to pass the house and even then, years after its loss, he had thought of it as his true home. When he told his mother he would take her away from Henley Street, he had always meant he would bring her here, to this part of Coldmouth where professional men and senior naval officers lived in a community separate from and indifferent to the town. He imagined she must long to return there as he did himself. In the old days she had had a great many friends who lived in red Edwardian houses like her own. The few who came to visit her after she left had been intercepted and snubbed by her husband, so they did not come again. Some tried to keep up an acquaintance with her by sending postcards from holiday towns and writing: 'Why don't you come for tea one day and bring little Hugo? Just say when.' She was a fool of a woman, but not without pride. The relationship of the pitying and the pitiful was not for her.

When Hugo said to her: "We'll go back there. We'll go right away from him. He won't even know where we are," it had seemed to him that in some little pocket of this street their old life awaited them intact. He saw it in his mind like a vision in a crystal; but she must have known better than he did.

The first thing Hugo did when he qualified as a teacher and was given his first appointment was to find a flat in this street. Change had set in here and the houses were being divided into flats that were easily let and at high rents. Hugo put his name down with a house agent who was an Old Boy of St. Aubyn's. They had never met before, but the agent recognised his responsibility toward Hugo and offered him the first free attic flat to be let at what he described as a low rental. Hugo took it, although, to him, the rent was frightening.

Now, among the jungle of bushes intersected by asphalt lanes that had once been streets, he looked for the situation of the house in which the flat had been. He had no idea where it was.

Pressing on against the cold, persistent wind, he came to

the next turning and read the street name placed on a post like a sign on a country road. The name, like those faces he sometimes passed, was at once familiar and forgotten. The flat must have been somewhere near here.

When he first told his mother he had taken it, she cried: "You can't go and leave me alone in this house."

"But you are coming with me," he said.

"Oh, no, no, no!" She turned from him as if he were mad. "That's impossible. I couldn't leave your father."

When he persisted, she said over and over again: "You don't understand."

At first it seemed nothing would induce her to come, and Hugo felt, like a stab of excitement, the relief of an ultimate escape—yet he could not escape so easily. To go without her would have been an admission of failure to overcome his father. The woman had been right in saying he had 'taken his mother away'. There would have been no point in going without her. He had bullied her, cajoled her, mesmerised her with persuasion and terrified her with pictures of what her life alone with her husband would be. Then, one Sunday morning when Mr. Fletcher was at church and Mrs. Fletcher still fluttered in indecision, Hugo had packed their belongings in an old trunk, fetched a taxi to the door and bundled her and the trunk into it. As they drove to East Coldmouth she had looked about her with a sort of demented guilt. When she got out her purse, wanting to contribute to the taxi fare, her hands had shaken so that she could not undo the clasp.

She had grown stout; her hands had grown rough; her purse and her clothes were shiny with age. As she heaved herself out of the cab and Hugo saw her, as for the first time, here, against the background of this long-desired neighbourhood, he felt brutal with rage against her. He had been mad to make her come.

He saw, and she saw, that the churches were coming out. Mr. Fletcher would be on his way home to find the letter Hugo had left. It was already too late for her to go back.

She trudged and panted up the three flights of stairs. She gazed at the two attic rooms with their scrappy furniture and windows that looked on to nothing, then she dropped to a chair and started to sob.

They had to share a bathroom on the first floor; the kitchen was an alcove on the second. All this cost £2 a week, more than half his wages.

"It's robbery," his mother sobbed. "Robbery."

Hugo, who had made every move with so cold a determination, hissed at her: "Shut up. The people in the flat below can hear everything."

At the venom of his tone, she dropped her face to her hands in an agony of tears.

He had never felt so defeated in his life before. He saw the flat for what it was, and wretchedly realised his mistake in coming here. He knelt beside her, trying to quiet her, and she clung to him with her fingers gripping his shoulders spasmodically, so that he kept saying: "For goodness' sake Mother, pull yourself together."

Somehow, after a while, she did pull herself together and unpacked their things and made the beds. She had for herself a room with a skylight, a room no bigger than a cupboard. Hugo had to sleep on a convertible sofa in the sitting-room. At that time he was meeting Tilly three or four times a week. The other nights he at first spent at home, but soon, having no room to himself, he felt the old need to get out, to wander the streets if he could afford nothing better. She complained bitterly of his absences. He urged her to go out herself, to pay visits or go to whist-drives, but the move had so jolted the structure of her existence she had lost her cheerful attitude toward the outside world. In Henley Street she had had the weekly church whist-drive where she had made a circle of friends. Among the crowd of women players there were usually a handful of men, retired and elderly, 'jolly old souls', 'fond of a joke, unlike your father', who paid her compliments and made her laugh. On her return she would describe to Hugo all the excitements of the game: how someone had trumped his partner's trick or she had had to play 'gentleman' or 'flirt twice'. It was an evening of extraordinary triumph when she came home with a prize, a tea-pot or a pair of sugar-tongs.

But all that was ended. She could not go there again. She had left her husband and Old Coldmouth would be 'talking'.

Hugo became impatient. "There are other churches and other whist-drives."

"I don't know the people. I don't know anyone here, now."

"You'll soon get to know them."

No, she would make no effort. Perhaps in the past she had merely reacted against misery, proving to herself and others that she had a right to enjoy herself. Now she had no right; she was wretched with guilt: but to Hugo it seemed she stayed in to punish him and he came near to hating her.

In his note he had given their new address, half hoping that Mr. Fletcher would pursue his wife and take her home again. But no word came from him. Then, one morning, a fortnight after her flight, Mrs. Fletcher paid a visit to Henley Street. She knocked on the door. No one answered it. As she passed the window she saw her husband watching out between the front-room curtains. He met her eyes, looked at her and through her, his face crooked in its bitter, unreal smile. He appeared not to recognise her; it was the smile of a blind man.

Hugo was in the flat when she returned, white-faced, dragging her feet, her whole air that of someone abandoned to despair. He had thought some frightful misfortune must have overtaken her. When she told him where she had been and what seen, he had been scarcely capable of speech. His anger broke out at last and he told her furiously that she was as foolish and irresponsible as a child.

She tried feebly to protest: "Don't speak to me like that, Hugo. Remember I'm your mother. Besides, you don't understand. You don't understand."

Not listening, he had reviled her like a maniac. When he paused from exhaustion she had been staring at him, her eyes swimming in tears. She stammered out:

"Why are you so cruel to me?"

"Because you've tortured me all my life with your stupidity."

She seemed to fall back before that accusation. It was as though her whole personality, will and hope fell back unable to fight. She put her hands up and covered her eyes, letting her tears flood between her fingers. Her despair frightened him. He did not know what to do for her. She was like a creature so stricken that one can do no more for it than hope it will soon die. He knew if he gave in to her he would be lost himself. He could not and would not give in. As a gesture he went out there and then, determined to stay out.

Later, when his anger had trickled away, he was wretchedly ashamed of himself, but he was still determined to follow his own will.

It was a few nights after that he had pushed Tilly into the arms of Webley. An insane action, he thought, and yet now it seemed an action to which he had been driven by an impossible situation. Not that it proved an immediate solution He had lost Tilly; his mother had remained. It had seemed she was on his hands for ever. Instead, he had escaped: and now even the attic flat in which they had lived so wretchedly was no more than a space in upper air.

Someone was coming towards him. He moved on quickly. The approaching figure passed under a street-lamp and was seen to be a policeman. On an impulse, as they were about to pass, Hugo said: "Excuse me." The police-man paused and Hugo asked the exact situation of the air-raid shelter which had been sealed up to form a common grave for the dead in it.

Despite the fact that Hugo was as tall as himself, the policeman, by curving back like a bow from heels to head, managed to produce an effect of looking down on his questioner. His face was a mask of self-importance.

"An air-raid shelter?" he echoed, frowning and pursing his lips.

"Yes, a large shelter; the main one round here. My mother was killed in it."

"Ho!" At this piece of news the constable allowed his posture to droop a little. "The thing to do . . ." he hummed and hawed and rocked on his heels. "The thing to *do* would be to find out who was the chief air-raid warden for this district. He'd know where the shelter was."

"You think everyone else has forgotten?"

"Well, I'm new here myself. It's been over some time now, the war. Past history you might almost call it. Things get forgotten." His voice dropped, then picked up with a consoling matiness. "They *should* have a list of wardens at the Public Library; or maybe at the Food Office. Or you might try the Police Station."

"Thank you."

The constable nodded, on his dignity again. Hugo walked on. He would enquire no more. Why, having been fool enough to return, need he make matters worse by picking over the débris of the past? He had had difficulty enough in escaping it.

When, acquitted and free, he had left the court and found that outside it he was condemned, he had gone about in a daze, his spirits defeated by the nagging injustice of his position. His power to hit back—that had really been a habit of hitting first—seemed to have deserted him. It had been his only weapon, and had brought him nothing but dislike: yet by losing it he gained nothing. He felt stupefied and helpless.

Before the accident he had been an eccentric, but he had been accorded a certain right to existence somewhere on the fringe of Coldmouth life. After his acquittal he had no right. People had been touched by the figure of old Lawson mourning the loss of his only son. They sighed over him, saying: "He is a broken man." By some alchemy of compassion 'Quids-in' himself had grown in memory to heroic stature. He was a first-class scrum-half, son of a city councillor, but, more, he had had the makings of a fine citizen such as Coldmouth could ill afford to lose. He was spoken of as a great and generous soul, grievously wronged by Hugo.

Hugo's acquaintances—at the best of times he could not have called them friends—had combined to exclude him from life. Even the kindest, no longer feeling need to excuse him, seemed to say by their glances: 'You have, with perverse determination, ruined your life here. Better go away.'

Or so it seemed. 'Better go away.' Yes. With the suddenness and force of a revelation, he knew that was the solution. He must turn his back on his familiar life. He must go to another country. To Egypt. Of course: to the P.I.

In his excitement—the excitement of a man presented with a miracle—he caught his mother's hands and kissed them, saying over and over again: "I'll find a job and then you'll come out and join me."

At first she had not taken him seriously, but when she realised he was determined to go, she cried: "You made me leave home. You brought me here, and now you abandon me. What am I going to do?" Her voice rose on the note of anguish that had tormented him in his childhood. He could not bear it. He shouted: "Stop that. Stop it at once," and she stopped, dumbfounded, with no idea what she had done wrong.

The prospect of escape now upheld him like intoxication in a sort of prolonged floating dream, carrying him over difficulties, above the housetops, keeping him even out of reach of his mother's repeated attempts to pluck him down. He was going. Nothing could prevent his going.

He had little idea how to set about getting the P.I. appointment. He could only suppose he must first get to Cairo. His trip to London had been, ostensibly, a visit in search of the student whose brother was in the P.I. This student had qualified as a teacher and been sent to a school at Sydenham, but Hugo arrived there only to find he had been transferred to Sheerness. That did not really matter. The days spent in London had been no more than a symbol of a new freedom.

He had had some idea of working a passage to Port Said but found no shipping company was interested in his services. He had to pay his way somehow. At last, unable herself to stand the strain under which he was existing, his mother admitted she had fifty pounds secreted in a Post Office Savings account, a remnant of her past wealth put away for a 'rainy day', and she gave him twenty, keeping thirty on which to keep going until he should send for her.

When all was settled he had been so excited that, coming face to face with Tilly in Ridley High Street, he had gripped her arm and cried triumphantly:

"What do you think . . .?"

But she had not listened. Snatching herself from his hold, she had said with quiet rage: "I have finished with you. I do not wish you to speak to me again. Never. Not on any pretext whatsoever," then she had swung away from him and crossed the road to a waiting car. Webley's car. Webley, at the wheel, turned his good-natured face and gave Hugo a pitying look. The car drove off.

Even that incident had not been able to depress Hugo's spirits. Indeed, it had gone out of his mind immediately.

He forgot about it until, years later, the war over and he settled in Menteh, the incident suddenly returned to overwhelm him so that it seemed an unbearable cruelty. It was then he discovered how a memory could become monstrous and break up through the mind like a black, uprisen shoulder to overthrow the structure of one's self-control. As in memory Tilly swung away from him again, he had broken down and wept. This ignominy, inflicted by the one person who had understood him, had been agony. Yet when he had stood in Ridley High Street looking after Webley's car, he had laughed and said aloud: "What the hell do I care?"

What the hell did he care about anything then? He had spent his last week or two in Coldmouth in a delirium. Could he have got away on the crest of it, his escape would have been perfect. But his mother had insisted on coming with him to Southampton and so spoilt everything. They had taken the slow, coastal train, changing at Brighton and Portsmouth. Hugo, as he watched the squares of hot summer sunlight creep about over the seats, had felt sick with impatience. If he could have speeded the train by adding his physical strength to the engine's force, he would have added it gladly. His mother, now in a state of settled despair, sat with a bleak look of anxiety on her face, questioning him every few minutes: Was he sure he had packed this or that? And he would not forget to do that or this? And when he arrived, he must let her know his new address. "Wire me," she kept saying, "don't forget to wire me."

At last he was safely on board: visitors were ordered ashore: he stood looking down to where she stood with the others on the quayside. She had been wearing a small straw

136

hat with artificial daisies and a veil. She stood with head bent, fumbling about in her bag. She found a handkerchief and pushed it up under her veil and mopped her eyes, then gazed at him bravely—she, who had been a darling only child, an heiress in a small way and a notable beauty in Coldmouth, had married a man no one liked, and borne a son no one liked, and now, shabby as a charwoman, had become a stout, bun-faced, featureless woman with little, wet, faded eyes, who had to make her way back to the empty flat; deserted; friendless.

He kept saying: "Don't wait, Mother. Do catch the earlier train back," but she waited until the end.

When the ship sailed, making the visible break with England, he had expected to feel a wild relief—but he felt no relief at all. Instead, when the quay was out of sight and he was able to turn from the rail and make his way among the strangers on deck, loneliness had come down on him like a paralysis of hope: but he faced it out. Freedom was loneliness, and freedom was what he had asked for. He had no cause for complaint.

His mother's first letter had reached him in August. She displayed a sort of quavering courage like that of a small child suppressing its tears. She was determined to follow him as soon as he was settled. He was saved from that by the fact that war broke out a few weeks after his arrival in Cairo. Their positions were suddenly reversed. He, young, healthy and reasonably capable, had been deprived by Army life of money and responsibility; while unemployables like his mother had been given the choice of any number of well-paid jobs. In no time she was serving in a canteen and enjoying herself immensely.

He had enjoyed himself, too. He had simply sunk back into acceptance of the laws, written and unwritten, that governed a soldier's life. He found himself without any enemies save those indifferent enemies who fired at him and at whom he fired back. In 1942 he had been wounded and sent to a hospital in Alexandria. When he was discharged, he was given a job as filing clerk at Cairo General Head-quarters.

Taking it all in all, the war had been the happiest period in his life.

CHAPTER V

ONE morning Hugo, driven from his own room by the
cold, went down to the Masters' Common Room.
Outside, rain fell from a foggy sky; it made the house dark.

As he passed the sitting-room, Hugo heard the Martyns
arguing inside. It was the first time, except for remarks they
had exchanged at meal-times, he had heard them talking
together. He paused in the hall. Their voices were low,
but Kyra's rose suddenly in a question, rhetorical, bitter and
accusing: "Isn't he all I have?" Hugo moved closer to listen,
but at that moment a light was switched on in Martyn's
study at the end of the passage. The door was open. He
could see Mrs. Prosser flicking at objects with a duster. If
she turned, she would see him. He moved on to the
Common Room and she, hearing his step, turned and said:
"Hello."

"Hello."

Hugo did not, as he would have done during his first
weeks in the house, retreat into the Common Room to avoid
her, but stood with his hand on the door, glad now even
of this contact with another human being. Mrs. Prosser
seemed equally glad to pause in her work.

Hugo said: "It's cold upstairs. I thought I'd light the gas-
fire in here."

"It's a cold house," she agreed. "Bitter cold. Like the

tomb. And damp, too. It's meant for big fires. You see the hall's got two fireplaces. That's the sort of thing. Big, roaring fires." Her eyes gleamed at the thought, but she added discouragingly: "And a houseful of servants to look after them."

"We're not likely to see those conditions again." Hugo followed the usual pattern of this conversation to ensure its continuance.

"No," Mrs. Prosser contributed wholeheartedly; she jerked a thumb over her shoulder: "*They* were the last lot to have all they wanted."

Hugo, taking this as an invitation, moved forward to get a closer view of the painting he had seen when he had talked in here with Martyn. "Mr. Martyn's grandparents?"

"Yes. Colonel and Mrs. Martyn. Edward VII paid them this visit and they had this garden party and someone made sketches; and then they had this picture painted. Mr. Martyn says it's a good likeness, but not a good painting, which doesn't make sense to me."

Hugo moved into the room, which was too small for the painting, and looked up at the two elderly people who gazed from another age, out of a frame so ornately massive that it seemed about to pull itself from the wall. The picture was as smooth-surfaced as a photograph.

Old Mrs. Martyn was standing on curved stone steps leading from house to garden—a great, corseted figure erect in satin, with yoke and dog-collar of lace, all richly held with pearls and brooches. She was covered with chains and short and long rows of pearls; she wore two roses, a bud and an open rose egg-fried flat on maidenhair fern. Above all this finery, spread on her bosom as on a jeweller's tray, her face was peevishly raised as though she were about to issue a command. Her hair was carried high from her face and surmounted by a large straw hat decorated with ribbons, ostrich feathers and the bejewelled giant heads of hat-pins. The wrinkles on the long gloves, the flowers on the silk stole, the pink lining to the stole, the fringes—all as exact as and more permanent than truth. Then from beneath the satin skirt hem, a boot of glacé kid: only the point of a toe, the first scalloped buttonholes round buttons that comprised a ring of brown about a golden eye.

Down on the grass, protecting his wife from a world against which she looked better armed than he, stood Colonel Martyn, his frock-coat buttoned tight across his lean, old body. The coat's dark V was outlined by the white V of the waistcoat, and this, with scarcely a thread of shirt showing, was filled by the flow of a broad black tie above which a collar, stiff and several inches high, held up the benevolent old face. Except for the white cavalry moustache, the face was almost Charles Martyn's face, but not completely, for beneath the grandfather's expression there was a certain habit of hauteur the grandson had never acquired. The striped trousers, though sharply pressed, were wrinkled by the bowing of the old horseman's legs, but the boots shone and were bespatted, and the hands that came from the stiff, white cuffs were white and smooth as cream.

Hugo was silent a long time, taking in every detail with a greediness of curiosity—the handkerchief peeping from breast pocket, the male buttonhole of rose and asparagus-fern; the beautiful curve of the stone steps that were rosetted over with lichen; and the hint of the room behind the open glass door.

Mrs. Prosser interrupted his preoccupation: "The colonel doesn't look a bad sort, but *her*! Asked for all she got, if you want my opinion."

"What did she get?" Hugo could not understand his own dislike of her criticism. What, after all, were the Martyns to him?

"She saw changes, she did, but it was thanks to her own extravagance. She wouldn't economise, not her. When the old chap died they found the place was mortgaged up to the hilt. Debts galore. All to keep her in the comfort she just had to have. Ten inside servants to look after those two old dears, to say nothing of all the outside help with gardeners, stable-men and the like. The old chap hadn't the heart to tell her the world outside was changing—prices higher, servants wanting living wages, taxes and rates and things. They were just going on the rocks. He died in time. He never had to tell her."

"So she was left penniless?"

"Not what *we* would call penniless."

Hugo flushed slightly at Mrs. Prosser's intimacy of tone, her assumption that he had grown up nearer to her world than to that of the Martyns. He was the more annoyed because she was right. How, he wondered, did he give himself away? She chattered on, unaware of his annoyance: "Those sort of people think they're poor if they can't have anything better than a flat in Park Lane. That's what she had when everything was sold up and the Death Duties paid. Mr. Charles married young the first time. He and his wife had a house in London, but the old girl wouldn't live with them. Not she. The part they lived wasn't smart enough for her. I bet he had a time keeping her going, the greedy, guzzling old trot! She never would believe the money had gone the way it had. She went a bit funny toward the end. Used to go and sit in Hyde Park and talk to people and tell them how her grandson had sold everything up and pocketed the money. Mr. Charles used to get letters from complete strangers telling him he was a wicked man and God would pay him out."

"How did you hear all this?" Hugo asked in a distant, discouraging tone that did not discourage Mrs. Prosser. She grinned at him amicably.

"My Miss Kyra tells me everything. This old trot," she jerked a thick, work-grimed thumb at the painting, "was still alive when Mr. Charles became engaged to Miss Kyra. Oh, she didn't like him marrying again. She couldn't see why he should. She said: 'He's got enough to do looking after me,' but she was pretty far gone then. Ninety-seven she was when she died. How they drag on, these useless old things! Take good care of themselves, of course. And all the time it was just moan, moan, moan about how life had changed. Yes, life *had* changed, and a good thing, I say. What had that old baggage ever done that she'd a right to be kept idle all her life? If you ask me, she just died out of cussedness. Passed away two days after Mr. Charles and Miss Kyra got married, and I don't think anyone cared much."

Hugo gazed at the couple as they stood in all their privileged 'rightness' and thought how he had once longed to be—well, not of that world: in his youth he had scarcely known such a world existed. No, he had not envied the Martyns; and those he had envied now meant nothing to him.

He turned and smiled at Mrs. Prosser and thought how change had come riding over life like a vast wave. One could be borne under by it; or strike through it like a strong swimmer and come out on the other side, shake one's head free of water, and go on.

And he—well, he was not done for yet.

Mrs. Prosser was still talking: "When she went there was nothing left, except a few pounds a week from an investment. Mr. Martyn still gets that: he can't touch the capital. He's supposed to hand it on to his heir, whoever that may be now. When he married again he had to find a job. He'd always lived very quiet, writing bits for magazines and so on, but still, you'd have thought a man in his position would have known people who could have got him something better than school-teaching! Something smart. You know, with a big oil firm or something, a job with money. But it seems he always had this fad for teaching. Miss K. wasn't pleased about it, as you can imagine."

"What happened to his father?"

"Oh, the father died young, killed in the Boer War. And the mother married again. She went to America. Mr. Charles almost never saw her. As for old Mrs. M.—I bet he didn't get much mothering from *her*. Queer, wasn't it, her blaming him about the money and his son doing it!"

"Doing what?"

"Embezzling."

"Embezzling!" said Hugo. "Stealing, you mean."

"Perhaps. But it wasn't Brian I blamed."

"Who did you blame, then? Pippin?"

"You know about him, do you?"

"Not enough."

"Oh, well. I've got to get on with my work." Mrs. Prosser's stream of talk broke off abruptly as though the sight of Hugo's curiosity were itself sufficient reason for not satisfying it.

He waited, thinking she might relent, but she ignored him; then, as he went without speaking again, she said: "Let's have a chat some time."

He looked over his shoulder and met her grin that she turned on him with such confidence she seemed to imagine it irresistible. He murmured, guarding against agreement or disagreement, then went into the Common Room and lit the gas-fire. As he felt its warmth, some of the edge left his gloom. He drew a chair up to it and settled down with his library book. Almost at once Mrs. Prosser tapped the door, opening it as she did so, and put her head round.

"Did you light it all right?" When she saw he had done so, she grinned and nodded, then entered, closing the door after her, and said with interest: "So you met Miss Kyra's brother, did you?"

"Her brother?"

"That Pippin you were speaking of. He's her brother. Didn't you know? We had him here at one time. That was a picnic, if you like."

Hugo got out his cigarette-case and offered it to her. She came over, rubbing her large, spatulate hands on her apron, and took a cigarette. He lit it for her and lit his own, then said: "Why don't you sit down?"

"Why not?" She sat on the opposite chair and stared directly at him with the perky attentiveness of a ventriloquist's doll. "Well, what did you think of Mr. Pippin?" she asked.

"I only had a glimpse of him. What did he do when he was here? Teach?"

"Teach!" She gave a derisive squawk of laughter that was an answer in itself. "I don't think he's ever done anything in his life—except he used to race cars. That's what finished him. He'd crashed two or three times; got his head injured, then they disqualified him. He didn't know what to do with himself; wandered about like a lost soul till the war came and he was called up. They sent him on a job down here and here he stayed."

"Is that why the Martyns took on Ridley?"

"In a way it was!" Mrs. Prosser looked disconcerted, as though uncertain how much Hugo knew. "Miss K. was worried about her brother, it's understandable. She couldn't get a word from him. Never knew what he was up to. It's true she may have said at times she'd be happier if she were here to look after him, but she never meant it. She never wanted to come here. Mr. Martyn ought to have known better."

"Still, he *did* come here for her sake?"

"I don't know, but I can tell you this: Mr. M. can blame himself for most of the trouble. If a man's a fool he has to take what he gets, I say."

"You mean you blame him for Brian's going off with the money?"

"Yes, I do," said Mrs. Prosser decidedly. "If he hadn't turned Mr. Pippin out none of that would have happened. He knew how attached Brian was to Pippin. I heard Mr. Brian crying while the row was going on and I heard him say: 'If he goes, I go too.' Well, if you ask me I say that's why he made off as he did."

"Do you think Pippin intended to join him somewhere abroad?"

"No good asking me. I don't know. They might have been up to anything, those two lads. But no one's heard anything from Mr. Brian; I'm pretty sure of that."

Hugo feared that was true. He changed to another line of enquiry: "So Mr. Martyn turned Pippin out, did he! Why did he do that?"

"Jealousy, if you ask me. Mr. M. spoilt that boy Brian, cosseted him like a girl; said he was the spit and image of his poor dead ma. Mr. Brian did just what he liked here. Then, when he and Pippin got great, the father didn't like it. In the end he turned Pippin out. It all happened suddenly, the only time I've seen the old boy show a bit of spirit. Miss K. was having a week-end in London at the time. Suppose that gave him his chance. Raging, he was. Said if Pippin wasn't out in half an hour, he'd call the police. Never heard anything like it. I was up in my room with the door ajar; heard every word. Pippin drifted off in the end. I saw him out of my window standing by the gate with his little bag. No idea where to take himself, poor soul. Then Brian ran out and they talked a bit, but Brian came back again. He liked his comforts, that young man. He stayed on till he got the cash."

"You think they arranged something?"

"Don't ask me. I know nothing. But when Miss K. got back—what a row! She's scarcely spoken to hubby since."

"And this unfortunate friendship Mr. Martyn mentioned to me? That was between Brian and Pippin, I suppose?"

"There was a bit of talk. People have nasty minds. They'd gossip about David and Jonathan these days." She glanced away as though the subject might interest others, but did not interest her. "Probably nothing in it."

"But what about the withdrawal of the grant? That finished Ridley. The grant wouldn't have been withdrawn for nothing."

"I couldn't say, I'm sure. I don't understand these things. I'm not one for gossip." She seemed to be smacking her lips over his eagerness for information.

He said irritably: "There must have been something in it."

"Well, there you are, you see. You know nothing about it, yet you say there must be something in it. That's how people's lives are ruined—by gossip and people thinking there must be something in it."

Hugo had no answer to that, but he said obstinately: "The grant could not have been withdrawn as a result of mere gossip."

Mrs. Prosser grunted. When she spoke she reverted to Martyn's errors: "He can blame himself, I say. He ought never to have taken this place. Him run a school! Why, he couldn't even run a whelk stall. All Miss K. wanted when the war was over was to go back to London. Nothing to keep them in Yorkshire. It was different when the war was on and nothing doing in town. Afterwards she wanted a bit of life. You can't blame her. She couldn't stick Scarborough." Mrs. Prosser looked inwardly, contemplating Yorkshire with a disgust which she expressed in four words: "Six hours from London."

"Why did they ever go there?"

"Not much choice, I don't suppose. Jobs were scarce in 1939."

"Were you in Scarborough with her?"

"What, me? No fear. I stayed in the theatre. I'd be there now, but when they took this place she begged me—yes, *begged* me—to come and give a hand. Well, I'm not as young as I was. I thought I wouldn't mind a settled job and a home; and I've always been fond of Miss K. She had bad luck."

"How was that?"

"Well, she had that success in *Message*, but it was too much of a success, you might say. People expected too much. The next play flopped and then she couldn't get a part to suit her—but she needn't have married *him*. Things weren't as bad as that."

"You think she married him in desperation?"

Mrs. Prosser sat upright. She gave Hugo a sharp glance; then, as though she were aware she had said too much, she began stubbing out her cigarette. Hugo knew he had heard all he was going to hear, but he made one more attempt to encourage her: "Mrs. Martyn and her brother are unusually devoted, aren't they?"

"Yes." She stared at the cigarette-end, drawing the word out and hissing a little as she did so. She murmured again, reflectively: "Yes," and then: "Of course they'd led a funny life, those two." She began to rise.

He put out his hand: "Don't go. Tell me about them."

"Curious, aren't you? I've got my work to do." She gave him a stern look, which she changed almost at once to a malicious smile: "Perhaps some other time. Keep your pecker up. Ta-ta-well," and she made her way from the room.

When he went in to the midday meal, she grinned at him

149

as though he were an old crony. Later she included him in her conspiratorial smile as she said to Martyn:

"This rain's coming through in a dozen places in the attics. My room's got a patch. I've put every pail and pan in the place up there. It's a bad thing getting the rafters soaked like that. You get dry rot in the rafters and you've had your chips. I'm telling you. And there's that damp getting worse in the kitchen. A lump of plaster fell off today as big as my fist. And to think you actually *paid* for the lease of this place."

"I took it at a bad time," said Martyn meekly.

"I'll say you did. And now the bathroom's fused. The whole place needs re-wiring. It'll be a mercy if we don't go up in flames."

"It might be a mercy if we did," muttered the headmaster, and Mrs. Prosser turned first to Kyra and then to Hugo a delighted and malicious grin.

Hugo frowned, angry for Martyn's sake and angry that she should regard him as an ally. He made up his mind not to talk with her again.

Martyn refused coffee and left the room. Later when Hugo went out to the hall he saw at the darkest end of the passage, beside the kitchen door, Martyn standing on a chair taking each fuse in turn from the fuse boxes. He was holding a candle and by its light his face had a patient intentness that moved a nerve in Hugo's throat.

After a day of rain a gleam came into the evening sky, the rain stopped and it was possible to go out. Hugo went thankfully, crossing the soaking lawn into the bare spinney and climbing up on to the downs, where the grey, coarse grass was pearled with wet. For the first time for a fortnight, he gave a glance to the Webleys' house. There it was, smug in its feather-boa of evergreens, its bare white flank blurred through the twilit damp. He imagined the life within it warm and comfortable; imagined a hand pulling heavy curtains to shut out the sight of the Channel waters that now had an iron edge, a look of perilous cold—then he returned down the horse-shoe of cliff flank to the esplanade. There was no bus waiting, so he started to walk towards the pier.

The wind came in gusts from the grey, slapping, chill-faced sea. In the western sky there was a break through which a yellow light fell to the promenade and ran along the black tarmac of the road. It touched the silver paint on the domes of the pier. One or two lights were switched on in the larger hotels, but there was not a human being in sight on the shuttered length of the front.

Of the summer's splendour nothing remained but the shelters spaced down the promenade, their elaborate iron-work painted cream, their cupolas silver to match the pier. These were unoccupied, of course—but, no; a girl was bunched in a corner of one of them. She had a sketching-pad on her knee and a paint-box was on the seat beside her. She sat sucking her brush and gazing out at the inhospitable sea; her side-face was neither pretty nor plain. A student from the municipal art school, he supposed; he'd seen them, self-consciously 'different', going into their school—a converted Congregational chapel—when he was at the Teachers' Training College. He passed her and forgot about her, then, when he was two or three hundred yards further on, he glanced back at her and was in time to see Martyn passing the shelter, looking in at the girl, then pausing to speak to her. In a moment Martyn had seated himself beside her.

Hugo turned and, keeping out of sight, walked back and sat on the shelter's other side. Back to back with Martyn and the girl, shut away from the roaring streamer of wind, he could hear the voices of the two echoing as in a sounding-box.

The girl was saying: "No, I can't say I ever saw him; not to my knowledge, that is."

She instinctively reflected Martyn's accents, yet could not drop the underlying Coldmouth whine.

Martyn said: "He was a good-looking boy, very like his mother. Yes, he was like her in every way. There was nothing bad about him, but I'm afraid he was a little weak. Gentle and weak. I thought we were so fond of one another. Even after he'd gone, I expected to hear from him. I was sure he would write when he could."

"Well, perhaps he will. When he's settled down in . . . where did you say he was going?"

"I don't know. He . . . he'd done something he shouldn't, you see. He just disappeared. The truth is he went off with someone else's money."

"Oh, dear!" the girl commented vaguely, then cheerfully added almost without a pause: "He'll write when he feels safe; you see if he doesn't."

"You think he will?"

Hugo heard this with some irritation, reflecting that safety for Brian meant for himself the certain loss of his money. There was a long pause on the other side of the partition, then Martyn said: "Now he's gone, I seem to have no one."

"Why, you've got your wife," said the girl with the demure cunning best calculated to clarify the situation.

Martyn said, sighing: "Brian was the son of my first wife."

"Oh!" The girl seemed satisfied by this reply.

Martyn said: "Would you like to stroll back to the house and have a glass of sherry?"

"Sherry!" she echoed doubtfully.

"A cup of tea, then?"

"I wouldn't mind a cup, but . . . well, no funny business."

"No. Certainly not."

The girl blew her nose. She sniffed and said: "Getting chilly, isn't it?" as though this excused a compliance she wished to be recognised as not usual. There were slight sounds as she gathered together her sketching materials, then they moved out from the shelter

Hugo watched through the glass screen as they went— the stooping, distinguished man, and the narrow, drooping girl. Martyn put a hand to her waist and moved round behind her so that he could walk by the kerb. The gesture had about it a protective tenderness that made Hugo think of Martyn's first wife and the little washes of grey and yellow that were her sketches of the river.

When Hugo first passed the girl, he had dismissed her at once as too tame and commonplace for him; not a girl on whom he would waste time. Now, as he watched the pair of them diminishing into the twilight, his old sense of loss came down on him. He sat still for a while, not eager to return into the wind, and as the evening fell he thought of the enduring river and the enduring sea, and the pathos of human mortality. What had it meant to Martyn?—the sight of this girl with her box of paints, this mortal engaged on recording the immortal, and having so little time for her work? To him she must have seemed above time's conventions. To Hugo she had meant nothing until he had seen her through Martyn's eyes. He had felt in her no importance against which he could pit his own. How few of his fellow men had had that challenging importance? With sudden and disturbing insight, he knew he believed in nothing. Seeing the human creature too dwarfed by space to have significance, he could feel no hope against that immensity. Now, for a curious moment, it seemed to him the very desire to encompass immensity was proof—of what? Of something known to Martyn, he was sure. He felt that in Martyn's forbearance toward these creatures there was proof that he saw and understood something hidden from Hugo.

Yet, if Martyn lived through compassion, why had he none for Hugo?

Hugo asked himself: "Am I outside the range of it?" and for the first time he felt less resentment than guilt, as though the fault were in himself.

He looked after Martyn. The twilight was deepening. The girl and the headmaster moved like shadows in the distance. Hugo jerked himself from the seat, and as he stepped out into the wind's discomfort his humour dissolved. Life seemed to him tedious, brief and without explanation. Why need he have suffered any of it? As for Martyn and the girl! Well, Hugo had no time to waste on girls like that. He had always wanted more than he could have. He had wanted more than Tilly. Indeed, when he first saw her, he had not wanted her at all.

He had met her at a Rugger Ball, the only one he ever attended. Someone had dropped out of a party, and at the last minute he had been asked to come as a partner for the odd girl. His ticket had been left for him at the Training College; he was to meet the others at the dance hall on the pier. When he opened the envelope and saw the large piece of gilt-edged pasteboard marked fifteen shillings, he thought: 'God, if they'd only given me the money instead.' He had had one shilling and sevenpence in his pocket and he knew that at some time in the evening he would have to buy his partner a drink. The ticket was marked 'Evening dress optional'—as though anyone in Coldmouth who owned an evening suit would dream of going to a Rugger Ball in anything else!

When he arrived, it seemed to Hugo that his shabby 'dark lounge', too short in legs and sleeves, was the only informal suit in the room. After a while he noticed others and their appearance disgusted him.

He had been told to come late but, having nothing better to do, he had not come late enough. There was no sign of the others. He hung round the entrance for a while, then, noticing a gallery that ran above one end of the hall, he decided to go up there so that they would not find him waiting for them when they came. The music changed as he climbed the stairs, and when he overlooked the hall the lights had been dimmed and a waltz flooded up from the band in a passionate crescendo. There was a man at the other end of the gallery turning a lime-light about over the dancers and changing its colour so that the women's shoulders were touched with sugar-pink and violet, gold and a blue like moonlight. Hugo went to the darkest part of the rail and, leaning over, tried to view the scene with contempt, but the music was too sensually disturbing for anyone as frustrated as he had been then. The violet lime-light passed over the whiteness of the girl's arms, lit the diamanté on their dresses and exaggerated their make-up so that the eyes that glanced up at him seemed deeply dark and drowsy with love. The scent of women warm with move-ment, the scent of their perfumes and powders clouding up to him, was unbearably sweet and exciting. His desire betrayed him so that he longed for one of these women—he did not know which. He followed with his eyes a fair-skinned, fair-haired girl with brilliants in her ears. Looking up once, she noticed him, and then each time she was turned toward the gallery she glanced up, half smiling, provoking him as though she felt his longing. But she was only one of them. He would, if he could, have possessed all the women drifting below him under the coloured lights on music and scent and the warm and heady air. As he watched the fair girl being swept by her partner to the furthest end of the hall, he saw his own party come in. He straightened himself, preparing to face them. He let them look about for him for some minutes, then he went down, made his way along the passage and entered through the end door as though he had just arrived.

By the time he reached the hall the music had stopped, the lights had come on and the dancers were walking back to their seats. He found his host, Binney, settling the party in a reserved alcove. They looked to Hugo as though they had just had a good meal somewhere. The two men, unlike most of the other men in the room, were not in dinner-jackets but in tails, with white bows prinked out and shoulders very square. Hugo eyed them amusedly from head to foot and said:

"God, you look like a couple of saxophone players."

Binney, a sober soul, known to his circle as a 'thoroughly decent sort', flushed and glanced at the girls as though Hugo had said something improper. One of the girls, a very pretty little blonde whose father was Coldmouth's best known auctioneer, tilted her chin towards Hugo with a smile of distaste.

The music was starting up again. He gripped her elbow and said: "Come and dance," and pulled her out to the floor before she could refuse. He had a sense of rhythm and danced well enough, but now he walked savagely about between the couples, treading on his partner's slippers and using her as a buffer against the crowd. She would have got away from him if she could, but he held her helpless and she could only spit out: "I warned Jim Binney against asking a guttersnipe like you"; at which he pushed her as though she were a handcart to the centre of the room, spun her round a dozen times and abandoned her, dizzy and fuming as she was, while he went over to a corner banquette and sprawled there alone for twenty minutes. At the end of this time Binney came over with his 'My dear fellow', apparently not choosing to speak of the incident with the blonde: "My dear fellow, Tilly's your partner. She's a stranger to Coldmouth, and doesn't know anyone here except us. If you don't dance, it's awfully awkward. It means the girls have to take it in turns to sit out."

He allowed himself to be led back to meet Tilly. He had

not noticed her in the group. When he met her, he was not impressed by her. Dark women had no attraction for him. Dutifully, he asked her to dance, and on the floor felt her in his arms cold and not desired. They danced a long time in silence before she said: "What made you like this?"

"Like what?" he sullenly asked.

"Maddening."

"Ha! Mirthless laugh!" Yet, in spite of himself, he was struck by the perception behind her question. Something had made him as he was. He had not been born a villain. He began contemplating the processes of change within himself.

When the music stopped and they stood clapping, he looked at her and thought this was probably the sort of girl for which he would have to be grateful. She did not excite him. She was too tall. She was too much of a real beauty with her narrow madonna face; not at all the sort of girl Coldmouth admired. If Hugo could have chosen he would have asked for a girl who would make him the envy of everyone—a blonde, of course, a dazzler, a girl dressed up to the eyes. Tilly's clothes had never been more than neat and inconspicuous: she made them herself.

They had danced together all evening. He offered her a drink and she asked for coffee. He got that for nothing from the buffet. His one shilling and sevenpence remained intact. It seemed to him she understood the whole situation and he liked her none the better for it. Did she expect him to be grateful? Well, he was not grateful. No one need shed tears over him. He wasn't a beggar.

For all that, they began meeting several times a week. She was the only person to whom he told anything of those years when, trapped between the insecurity of his school and the insecurity of his home, there had been no place where he could relax guard. During the months they went round together, he must have told her everything there was to tell.

In response she would shake her head, touching his hand suddenly and intimately as though it were in his flesh that he had received vital injury. He despised pity and yet, receiving it, his defences became meaningless.

She asked him: "What were you like before you moved to Old Coldmouth? Can you remember?"

He recalled himself as a gentle, trusting child, one for whom the foundations of the world were to be shaken by the fact that he could speak the truth and be unbelieved. Worse, he could be persecuted for speaking the truth. . . .

She had said: "You might have been quite a different person, differently treated." Because of that he had imagined she would forgive him anything. Probably she had forgiven him much. He could not remember. But he remembered that when he had felt most for her, he had never felt violently. He had recognised her quality. No other woman would be so forbearing; no other attempt to understand him— always supposing he wished to be understood.

The truth was, he suspected she was a little smug with him. She too had been struck by the profundity of her question. This 'understanding' had become a sort of bond. Whenever they had nothing better to talk about, they could discuss his early days. She was never bored. On the contrary he began to suspect she was too interested. He became convinced she was formulating some plan to reform him—and when she had reformed him, of course, she would finish with him. Why not? What would be left for her?

If he had often reacted brutally to her, it had been as a protest. And, more than all that, he did not want what he had not asked for. He wanted what exhilarated him—the antagonism of that fiendish little blonde. To have overcome her would have been a triumph. Even now, feeling a salacious pleasure at the thought, he started to smile to himself. . . .

And, smiling, he glanced self-consciously about him and saw the bus coming. He ran to the next stop and caught it. Darkness had fallen. Sitting on the front seat, looking into the black nothingness of the sea, he remembered that on the night he had realised Tilly was lost to him he had walked down the steps to the shingle. He had thought he would walk straight into the water and drown. He didn't, of course. He had stopped when he reached the frill of wave that came in from the blackness and was touched by the esplanade lights just before it broke. He was not free to die. He could not leave his mother alone in the flat to which he had taken her. Because of her, he was forced to live on, and he told himself he hated her for it. If he had had no mother there would probably have been some other excuse. He had lived; yet, the fact remained, he had wanted to die.

He had lost what he supposed he did not want, and because of that he had wanted to die.

More fool he!

She had cajoled him out of hiding, had stripped him of his natural defences, had dared to pity him and then, at the first excuse, had abandoned him. "I don't want to speak to you or see you again." What, he wondered, had she told

Webley about him? What had she told the rest of them? If he knew nothing else, he knew what she had said in the witness-box to prove him capable of the irresponsibility that could result in manslaughter.

He thought suddenly and savagely: 'I would like to slap her face.'

'I would like to murder her,' he thought and felt a deeply sensual and nervous excitement at the thought Tilly's murder could wipe out, as nothing else could, the memory of her rebuff. That would end her and end himself. That would end memory. As for Webley—what had it to do with Webley, anyway?

The excitement faded, and he was still alive. The evening stretched before him as empty as the universe.

When he reached the harbour the public-houses were still closed. He walked up and down waiting for them to open. He had drawn some money from his account a few days before and now only five pounds remained in it. When that went he would not have even the refuge of the public-houses.

At the back of his mind was the belief he would meet Kyra somewhere down here. As soon as it was open, he went to the Harbour Bar and took his drink to the seat which he had shared with her and Kinky Bluett. It was again Saturday night; the bar was filling quickly, and within an hour he was almost crowded off the end of his seat. He felt it useless to stay longer. Even if she came now there would be no place for her to sit with him. He moved on to a small public-house a few doors along. The first person he saw there was Kyra standing alone at the bar. She turned her head as he entered and their eyes met. She made no attempt to hide her disappointment that he was not the person she was expecting. She seemed scarcely to recognise him until he smiled, then she gave a wry smile as though to say: 'You know I am disappointed. Very well, I am disappointed.'

He went straight to her: "I thought I might see you around," he said.

When he had bought his drink she replied, her tone a comment not a provocation: "I should not have thought you got much change out of seeing me."

He replied with an equal candour: "I am glad to see anyone to whom I can talk."

She narrowed her eyes a little; he expected a snub but, after a moment, she said only: "I suppose you haven't seen Pippin anywhere about?" When he shook his head, she added: "I was to meet him here at six. This clock must be fast." The clock said twenty past seven.

"It is fast," Hugo agreed.

"Let's sit down."

Hugo followed her over to a wooden form against the wall. She sat with nothing to say, her spirit seeming keyed down to a mournful evenness and silence. He asked her at last: "Why do you worry so much?"

She answered simply: "Saturday night is trouble night."

"Did you find him that last time I was with you?"

"No." After a long pause, she asked: "Have you no friends in Coldmouth?"

"I never had any."

"Not even a girl?"

"Yes, I had a girl once. She married someone else."

"Oh, is that why you went to the ends of the earth? And

162

why have you returned? To come face to face unexpectedly? To look at her with reproach? To bring a blush to her cheek?"

This was so near the truth, it brought a blush to Hugo's cheek. At the sight of it, Kyra burst out laughing. Hugo said: "If we are exchanging confidences, there are several things you could tell me."

"Are we exchanging confidences?" She looked away, no longer laughing. "You are curious about my brother?" (Her use of the word 'curious' made him wonder what Mrs. Prosser had told her.) "He was a racing driver. He had an accident at Brooklands before the war and the result is he has become a bit—what? Disorientated. He was all right during the war when he had a job and was working under orders: he was, as a matter of fact, rather good. He's no fool. He broke German naval codes, and did it damned well. But when the war ended, the job ended. I knew he'd be lost again. I wanted him to come and live with us. Charles was teaching at Scarborough then. I couldn't get down here very often, and Pippin wouldn't reply to my letters. We had a week-end here once or twice, but couldn't get much sense out of him. He'd picked up with the usual crowd—that Kinky Bluett was one of them; he's a buyer in a woman's hat shop. I knew I'd never winkle Pippin out of this place. I was worried, but not enough to justify Charles's taking on Ridley—that was lunacy." She stopped, bit her lip in, then, turning on Hugo, said with a half-humorous insolence: "What else do you want to know?"

"What else do you want to tell me?"

She gazed reflectively before her and said after a moment: "I don't think I have anything else to tell."

He felt now, having gone so far, he might as well go further; he said: "Tell me how you came to marry Charles Martyn. There must have been a time when you could have married almost anyone."

"Yes, there was. But I let it go past. I only wanted one thing then—a great career."

"I don't understand what prevented it. I thought you were wonderful in the *Message*, yet Mrs. Prosser said . . ."

"Oh, Mrs. Prosser's been talking, has she?"

"She didn't say much."

"Only that I flopped in every other part I got?"

"She said you had bad luck."

Kyra made no comment, but after a moment said: "Anyway, in the end I married Charles. I used to think I could have done worse. Still, it's too late to worry. My life's finished. I have to accept that fact." She tilted her glass in her hand and stared into it.

"You don't really believe that?"

"Do you imagine I'm still kidding myself a glorious future lies ahead? I'm at the age when life begins to show results. If the results aren't what you hoped for, it's just too bad. It's too late to start again."

Her disconsolate resignation did not convince him. He felt he was being called upon to deny all this, and when she came to a stop, he denied it fervently, speaking out of a very considerable ignorance of his subject.

"I think this is all nonsense. I've always heard you could start on the stage again however late in life. All sorts of people have done it. They have to have actresses to play older parts."

"That's true," she agreed, seeming to hold back her own

164

eagerness. "Some people have no success until they're old enough to play character parts. I suffered more than anything from not finding a part to suit me. I had to take what was offered. One can't rest for ever—but these silly simpering girl parts. I just felt bored in them."

Talking, she talked herself into a different mood, and her voice rose with her excitement: "Perhaps I'll do something yet."

"Have you thought of returning to the stage?"

"Thought about it! I think of nothing else." She gave a sort of wild gulp of laughter so that Hugo was uncertain whether she was to be taken seriously or not.

Before he could ask her anything more, she was distracted by the opening of the door. Pippin entered behind two bluejackets.

"At last!" she said loudly with theatrical exasperation, but Pippin did not hear her or look in her direction. He went to the bar with the sailors, one of whom was behaving toward him with offhand rudeness. The other, the younger, kept in the background as though unwilling to associate himself with his companion's conduct.

Pippin spoke to them quietly. The offhand sailor, looking round to gather applause, replied at the top of his voice: "What will I drink? Very generous, I'm sure. Hey, Jackie-boy"—he turned upon the second sailor—"here's a bloke wanting to buy us a drink. What d'you think his game is, eh?"

The second sailor replied quietly, but had scarcely got his words out before his companion shouted him down: "But I don't like it, see! I don't like it."

"You don't have to like it." Kyra strode forward, her

face distorted with anger, and caught Pippin's arm. "Come over here," she ordered him, and he came, smiling vaguely, unmoved both by the sailor and by Kyra's prancing fury.

"That's right, lady," the sailor called after her, "take him away and slap him."

Kyra, ignoring this, pushed Pippin down to the form as a mother pushes down an irritating small boy. She said: "I've been waiting for you since six o'clock."

"Oh, my dear!" Pippin put both his hands into Kyra's and gazed contritely into her face. "I am *so* sorry. I forgot. I simp-ly forgot."

"What have you been up to?"

"Nothing, my dear, nothing, I assure you." He gazed past her and smiled at Hugo. "Who is your charming friend?"

Kyra introduced them.

"How nice!" said Pippin. "I adore meeting new people. I do hope you are staying for a long time. Will you have a drink?"

"Have you any money?" Kyra asked.

"Not a penny." Pippin smiled round in delight at his own reply.

"All right!" Without further comment, she turned to Hugo and asked: "What will you have?"

"Have this on me," he said.

"No." She had a sort of irritable insistence that was not displeasing and in the end it was she who bought drinks, and sandwiches as well.

While she was at the bar, Pippin gazed into Hugo's face and said: "So you are living in that wretched house! How dreadful for you! I could not stand it; simply could not stand it. And without poor Brian there, how grim it must be! He was such a nice boy! So handsome, and so nice! A sweet boy!"

"Have you any news of Brian?"

Pippin answered without surprise or hesitation: "No news, alas!"

"You expect to hear from him?"

"Once he was safe, I hoped to hear. Why not? A message of some sort. Just a word. He could have used some other name."

"Where do you imagine he has gone?"

Pippin seemed about to reply, then shook his head instead, all the time smiling his steady, gentle smile.

Hugo, seeing Kyra had been served, went to the bar to carry the drinks—beer for him, gin for herself and Pippin, and a plate of sandwiches. Her mood had changed. She sat between the two men and, talkative and elated, took charge of the conversation. She said to Pippin: "Mr. Fletcher thinks I should return to the stage."

"But of course, my dear," her brother said vaguely.

"And you? What would you do if I went to London?"

He smiled at her with a tender sweetness and put his hand on her arm. She turned to Hugo and said: "Until I married, Pippin and I were never really separated. We would not have been then, really, but Charles got this job in Yorkshire, and Pippin refused to come with us. I almost stayed in London because of him, but the war was hanging over us. Yorkshire seemed the best place. When Pippin was conscripted he was sent down here." She glanced round at Pippin. "You were very clever, weren't you, darling?" She patted the hand that still rested on her arm, and turned again to Hugo. "My brother broke one German code after another. They said he was invaluable."

Pippin continued to smile, but his attention began to wander. His hand slid from his sister's arm and he looked to the bar. The sailors were drinking beer, the noisy one still noisy, the other glancing about until he met Pippin's eyes. Pippin lifted his eyebrows a little. Hugo noted the tremor of understanding between him and the young sailor.

Kyra was eating sandwiches and saying: "Pippin and I were inseparable before my marriage. Well, we had a good time once in our lives, if we've had precious little since. Isn't that so, darling?" Pippin, drawn back, smiled agreement, then looked away again. "Everyone adored Pippin. I suppose there is nothing worth doing we have not done; no one worth knowing we have not known. Oh!" She threw out her hand to express the wonders of their past: "What does it matter how we live now, we lived well once. Yes, we knew how to enjoy ourselves."

Hugo wondered if Kyra were already drunk. He made a murmur of interest and she went on, describing those enviable days when she was a successful actress and Pippin a famous racing driver. That was the life! That was the world to which they belonged! How on earth did they ever get doomed to this place?

Pippin, when required, turned his smile in agreement, but in the middle of one of her sentences he murmured: "So sorry, darling; must go now." When Kyra put her hand on his arm to hold him he settled back for a moment, but, cunningly, as soon as her attention was elsewhere, he slid along the form until he was near the door; with a slight gesture at the young sailor, who lifted one finger in response, he rose in a movement noiseless and skilled. He smiled at Hugo, a smile that had the flattering quality of trust shown by an animal or child, and made his escape.

He had been gone a full minute before Kyra became aware of the emptiness beside her, then she started round and stared, amazed, at the door. For her he had simply disappeared.

"When did he go?" she demanded of Hugo.

"Just this minute."

She seemed at a loss, but got to her feet and said, as she had said the last time: "I must go after him."

"Oh, why?" Hugo was annoyed.

She did not answer. He looked after her as she went and said to himself: "What a couple!" No wonder Martyn had thrown Pippin out. As for Kyra's devotion to her brother, it was less a devotion than an obsession, a need to dominate, a . . . Hugo did not know what it was, but he told himself he despised the whole set-up. Whatever his own faults, he was better than those two, anyway.

Yet . . . whatever he told himself, he was alone again. As he finished his beer and ate the last sandwich, he watched the two sailors. The noisy one had not stopped talking since they came in. The young one glanced once or twice at the door, then, when his companion paused to breathe, he murmured something.

"Oh, no, Jackie-boy," shouted his companion. "No, you don't. You're standing your round."

The young sailor bought a pint of beer, and as his companion tilted back to drink it, he slid through the door and was gone: "Hey, hey, Jackie-boy!" the other bawled, but there was no reply. He finished the beer and went. The bar was empty except for Hugo.

Slowly finishing his own drink, he contemplated his solitude and saw himself as an actor without a part in life. The others might have a word for him in the wings, but they dropped him as soon as their cues came. If he wanted to live, he had to return to the past when, if he had done nothing else, he had suffered. It seemed to him that only there could he find any sort of life. Now he did not even suffer.

When his glass was empty, he saw no reason for staying. He drank only in hope of company, and there was no company here. He wandered out.

A distant clock struck nine. The dead hour of nothingness. From habit he moved towards Ridley, but was unwilling to return there. Now, neither late nor early, a time without hope either of beginning or end, the house would be intolerably empty. Kyra was out. Mrs. Prosser always disappeared somewhere on a Saturday night. Probably Martyn, finding he had the place to himself, had given his girl supper and would now be walking her back to Coldmouth. Even if he were at home, there would be little hope of his seeking out Hugo's company.

And there was not only tonight, but all the other nights. Hugo asked himself how much longer he would be able to bear his own inactivity. He knew he should move to rooms in Coldmouth now and start looking for a job, any job that would give him a wage and a right to exist. But to do that would simply be an announcement that he gave up hope of repayment. He would never hear from Martyn again, he was sure of that. It would be the end. He felt an obstinate anger at the thought. He'd be damned if he'd give up so easily.

He turned off to the left. This was the bleak hinterland that led to Old Coldmouth. Finding it bleaker even than his memory of it, he veered eastwards and in spite of himself moved towards Ridley. He thought of going to a cinema but it was late, and in Menteh he had lost the habit of cinema-going. In any case, he had never found much compensation in shadows.

Now he was in streets still haunted by his youth. He had always taken a diagonal route home this way. He passed small shops which he had forgotten and now remembered with painful acuteness, and saw ahead the light of the Cold-mouth Police Station. That brought to mind something he could do. He entered the police station. A corporal was on duty. Hugo said he was looking for the site of the air-raid shelter which had received a direct hit and been sealed up. He explained that his mother had been among the dead inside it.

The corporal had heard of such a shelter but could not say where it was. "Now, the man you want is a Mr. Trike. Yes, T-R-I-K-E. He used to live around there, but he moved his wife out before things got too hot. Lucky for her. She went to the country, and Mr. Trike just settled in at the A.R.P. centre. He was in charge, y'see. And after the war . . ." the corporal stopped, then called to someone in the next room: "Hey, Cliff, where did the Trikes move to after the war? Gent's enquiring."

Hugo left at last with an address in a street off the esplanade. It was a mile away. Propelled by a sense of purpose, he set out to find it. When he found it, he learnt only that the Trikes had moved.

The new tenant, a stout, coatless, collarless man who

shouted up from the basement, thought they had gone to a private hotel—the what-do-you-call-it. The Ridgway. Were they still there? He couldn't say.

Hugo went on. He knew the Ridgway, a small residential hotel in Ridley, a remnant of village days. It had once been very smart, white-painted with a basket of pink geraniums hanging within a Georgian porch, but it had grown shabby since the war. Even now, with its down-at-heel look, it seemed a pleasant place, and he was glad of an excuse to enter it. The hall was covered with torn rugs, and lit by imitation candles. Hugo waited several minutes before a girl appeared. She, hearing the name of Trike, said: "Half a mo'," and ran straight upstairs.

A woman came down: "I'm Mrs. Trike," she said in a breathless, lisping way, bending forward anxiously. "Do you wish to see me?"

"No, I asked for Mr. Trike."

"Oh! I'm afraid you can't see him. Oh, no. He has passed on."

Hugo looked uncomprehending.

"He's dead." Her voice seemed full of wondering complaint at the fact. She stared at Hugo as though he might have a useful suggestion to make.

Hugo said: "I'm sorry. I wonder . . . it's just possible you might know . . . you might be able to help me."

"Come in here." She led him into the hotel sitting-room, where there were a great many chairs and sofas covered in washed-out chintz. She motioned him to sit down and said: "Now!" smiling as though some pleasurable entertainment were about to begin.

While Hugo explained what he was seeking, her

anticipation drooped and when he had finished she sat downcast. "Well, I did hear about it," she said vaguely. "Yes, my husband told me. I was away at the time. I went to the country. There was nothing I could do here; I'm not very strong, so my husband thought I ought to go."

She was in early middle age, a soft-looking, pallid woman, but by no means fragile. She sighed, then brightened a little to say: "I wish I could offer you something to drink, but this is a temperance hotel."

Hugo thanked her and assured her he did not want a drink. He leant away from her, repelled by her quality of acute loneliness. His instinct was to escape at once, but he was held by the certainty she knew where the shelter was. He knew he could do much as he liked with her but he must be careful to remain uninvolved in the doing. She mumbled on:

"It's pleasant to have a little something now and then; in moderation, of course. I never think anyone, even gentlemen, should indulge to excess. Still, each to his little pleasures is what I say. But it's awkward for ladies—those who've been brought up like me, I mean—otherwise I'd ask you to come out for a drink. There's a very nice public-house near here kept by a lady known to me."

Hugo, feeling it required of him, suggested she might like to come and have a drink with him.

"Oh, dear," she said, "I didn't mean. . . . Oh, no, I couldn't accept . . ." and after some flurries and delays, she put on a hat and coat and came out.

When he got her into the street, he started walking towards Coldmouth. The lights of the near-by Ridley Arms shone brightly across the street. She made an ineffectual movement towards them, but Hugo said: "I know a nicer place."

As they passed into the darkness of the lower High Street and saw ahead the barren blackness of the bombed area, her pace slackened. "Such a long way," she breathed and yet followed, unable, in her loneliness, to break away. As the wind burst on them over the empty sites, she began to speak in a whimpering voice:

"Really, my husband should have thought of me. He knew how much a woman needs a little pampering. He always had to take care of me. How could he leave me alone like this?"

"What happened to him?" Hugo asked, to keep her going while they crossed the frontier into desolation.

"He overdid it. He worked for others, and now I'm left all by myself. Everyone said what a good sort he was, but they didn't stop to think I was the one who paid for it."

"What was the trouble?"

"I don't know. No one really knew. I got back in '44 when things had quieted down. People said to me they saw a change in him, but I thought he seemed much the same. He had his ups and downs; we all do. One night, when he was a bit low, he started telling me about things he'd seen in the raids. They used to bring him arms and legs and so on— things they'd found—he had to try and identify them. One night it was the top half of a baby without an identity disc. The hand had been blown off. It got him down, he said. I said: 'Now, you've got to put that right out of your head. The war'll soon be over and we all want to forget about it.' Stay cheerful's my motto, so far as you can. It's no good brooding on things. I said: 'I'm not well myself. You ought to think of me.' We'd got a maisonette then, a nasty, damp place; not like the nice little flat we lost in the blitz. Everything gone, even the dog, poor thing! Now, that *did* upset me. The maisonette wasn't healthy, and it was a lot of work, so we moved into the Ridgway. The Ridgway's what you'd call snug, and we got a very special price because Mr. Trike had done the manager a good turn. Yes, it was very nice moving there. We could be having the time of our lives now. He had a small pension—a Warrant, he was—and he had his job with the Building Society and we'd a nice bit saved. Why, what with no children and nothing to do, we could've been happy as the day is long. But he would mope. In the end they said he'd got pneumonia. He'd had flu bad, it's true, but I don't know. I think it was this brooding did it. All the time he was delirious he was going on about the raids and things he'd seen. If you ask me, he didn't want to live." Her tone was less a mourning than an accusation of the dead.

Hugo asked: "How do you manage now? Have you a job?"

"A job? Oh, no. I'm not very strong. The Building Society was very decent. Gave me a nice little annuity— and quite right, under the circumstances. Bert was killed by the war just like them in the front line. And, of course, we'd a nice bit saved and the manager at the Ridgway's very good, but it's lonely."

Now her story, which she must have told so often, was finished, it was as though a link had been broken between her and her listener. She became aware of how far they had walked, and became peevish: "Where *are* we going?"

"I thought first you might show me where that air-raid shelter was."

"What!" she was startled enough to show indignation. "You want to wander about in this dismal place! Why, it's like a graveyard," but they were already in the centre of the bombed area and there was nothing else she could do now but return alone to the hotel.

"Now, where is it?" Hugo asked, feeling that in his ruthlessness he was getting his own back on something, though he did not know on what. She looked about her miserably. He realised she was a little afraid of him and that increased his satisfaction. She said: "I think down here."

They turned into a side street where the cellar pits were full of bushes. She peered about nervously, resentful but hoping, perhaps, to get her drink in the end.

"I think it was here. It was under the road, I know that."

At first he doubted her. He thought she was trying to get the search over and done with—and yet he was not sure. They were standing on a heavily cemented oblong, about ten foot across and fifteen foot long, set partly in the gravelled pavement and partly on the road. It certainly looked like a large tomb-stone. If it were not the shelter, it would be difficult to say what it was.

Looking round at the sea mist creeping in among the bushes with their fronds of dead flowers, he supposed he would never know for certain where his mother was entombed. And why did he want to know?

To Mrs. Trike he said, as though releasing her from a task: "All right," then added: "Thank you very much."

He led her to the esplanade and turned into one of the more expensive hotels. The public rooms were poorly lit, cold and deserted, but he could see she was gratified. She asked for brandy and, feeling she had earned it, he ordered her a double.

She chattered happily about the pleasures of life in hotels, but Hugo had nothing to say. He was sunk in depression, wondering why he had been so determined to find the shelter. Could his visit matter to the dead? Whatever he did now, he did too late.

He looked across at Mrs. Trike and saw her face break into a foolish smile as the drink warmed her.

"It was kind of you to come," he said, "but I need not have troubled you. It was a waste of time. We can't bribe the dead."

"Ah, what do they care?" she gaily asked.

At the thought of their indifference, he became filled with longing for the oblivion that must come at last.

CHAPTER VI

AS November set in, a sort of permanent fog of cold filled the house so that the walls and woodwork had the icy dampness of a toad. Even in the sitting-room, when the fire was lit, a haze dimmed the surfaces of furniture and glass, and a blue dimness filled the furthest corners. The windows had probably not been cleaned since the school's failure. They were so murky, the interior of the house was dark by early afternoon.

The gloom and discomfort of English winter turned Hugo's thoughts more and more often to Egypt's brilliant heat. At times as he lay on his bed, bundled up in his down quilt, he experienced again with such vividness the incidents of his Menteh life that he would return to the present aghast, like one who wakes up in a grave.

He began to believe he had lost something dear to him in losing his Menteh life; that he had known there, in the evening companionship shared in Abdul's garden, a form of happiness—yet, when he seized upon and examined separate incidents, he was troubled because they did not confirm his belief. When he recalled his last evening in Menteh, his farewells, his departure, he tried to recall them with regret— but his memory refused him deception. In his mind he sorted his movements of that evening, seeking something he could not find.

Abdul, who owned a car, had driven him to Assuit to catch the Cairo train. At first the others had been coming with them. It was to be a night out, a 'spree', as Père Legouis had called it; but, at the last, Aston's wife had persuaded him not to go, and Père Legouis began to have doubts about the wisdom of spending a night—for the journey to Assuit and back would take the whole night—away from the Mission. Only Abdul made no excuses. Between Hugo and the other two a rift seemed to have opened. He felt in them no regret at his going, but only an edgy annoyance as though he were letting them down.

Père Legouis had said: "Forgive me, dear friend, forgive me; but duty must come before friendship," and Hugo thought: 'Always the same old humbug.'

Aston had said: "England! The weather, the food, the fuel shortage; and, oh! the income tax! Rather you than me, dearie!" but it was not with pity he had bent and gazed into the car as Abdul and Hugo drove off. He waved after them, shouting: "Hope the boat sinks!" and it was not altogether a joke. It occurred to Hugo then that Aston had never liked him. In Coldmouth he would have recognised that dislike at their first meeting. In Menteh he had remained unaware of it until the last. He knew his imperception had resulted not from Aston's clever dissimulation but his own indifference to the feelings of anyone in Menteh. That indifference had been his happiness.

He had parted from both his friends without a pang. What did he care? Unless he were to be exceptionally unlucky, he would never see either of them again. Abdul, as an oriental, had, whether Hugo realised it or not, been closer to him and more remote. The closeness had come from a simpler response; the distance from the ultimate differences of race. As they drove away, Abdul said: "They should have come with us. It was not kind to an old friend."

Hugo had wriggled slightly under the candour of this censure that might more tactfully have been left unexpressed. "It doesn't matter," he said.

"But I think it does matter," said Abdul, righteous as ever. "They may not see you again."

Hugo knew that was exactly why Legouis and Aston had not felt it necessary to come. The final line had been drawn across the balance sheet of his friendship with each. What point in giving Hugo a credit he could not be called upon to repay?

Feeling a slight bitterness at the thought, he put it behind him, repeating: "It does not matter," with a conviction that persuaded even Abdul.

The road ran between the river and the cultivated land. The flat river surface and flat fields were flooded with the blue-white ice light of a full moon. Hugo could see, a long time before reaching them, the half-dozen standing columns of the Temple of Menteh. At the thought he would never again see the temple he was filled with grief. Tears came to his eyes. His departure seemed to him scarcely bearable. He had visited the temple three, perhaps four, times during his years in Egypt, yet it was as though he were leaving something more than a friend. He watched it approach, saw the moonlight pick out the bulls' faces on the capitals, and was preparing to turn in his seat and look directly at it, so that it would remain for ever in his mind, when, as they passed it, Abdul spoke, distracting him so that he forgot it until it was out of sight. Probably the temple prompted Abdul to say:

"In England you have many great and beautiful buildings, yes?"

"I suppose we have. There's Westminster Abbey and St. Paul's . . ." Hugo might have achieved a considerable list of London's chief buildings but he realised Abdul was waiting to say more. When he paused, Abdul sighed heavily.

"How I have longed to see such things! Imagine, in all my life I have been only in Egypt! Cairo is a nice city, of course, very nice—but I want to visit such a city as London where there are great rivers and many mighty mountains. How is the snow, now? Very cold, eh?"

So, during the two hours' drive to Assuit, Abdul described from his imagination the great northern capitals of Europe, making pictures Hugo did not attempt to correct. What did it matter? Abdul's sugar factory, that somehow kept him, his wife and six children, his mother, three sisters and a brother, could never afford him the disillusionment of travel. Abdul was still talking when they reached the station at Assuit and walked up and down the empty platform, the moonlight glancing beside them along the rails. The sophisticated train with its streamlined locomotive, its dining-car and *wagons-lit*, fussed in at last, bringing an odd smell of another world.

"Good-bye, dear friend." Abdul gripped his hand. "I shall see you one day in England. Write to me that you are happy." And he had stood, white-suited, waving a white handkerchief in the moonlight, as the train carried Hugo into the future and left him behind in the past.

A tap on the door of his room startled Hugo to

consciousness. He called irritably: "Come in," and Mrs. Prosser entered with an electric fire.

"*He* sent it up," she said. She plugged in the fire and watched the single bar turn from black to geranium-red, then she swung round on Hugo: "What's this?—you telling Miss Kyra I've been talking about her?"

"Why!" Hugo struggled up and stared half-sleepily at her. "It was the barest mention . . . I've forgotten what was said, but I certainly said nothing you need worry about. She was simply telling me about the wonderful life she and Pippin lived in London, and . . ."

"*Her!* Her and that brother of hers! Wonderful life, indeed! That's what she'd like you to think. She had that one success, I admit it. She had a glimpse of high times, right enough, but after she kept flopping, the invitations dropped off quick. They always do. She knew she'd had it when she married him."

Hugo remained silent, letting her talk, feeling a shameful pleasure in this betrayal of Kyra, yet not wishing to be involved in it.

"She thinks she was in the thick of it, but, believe me, she wasn't more than on the fringe. Now, at one time, I was lady's maid to the Honourable Mrs. Keith Clarkie as was—she'd had three other husbands since then—and the money that woman spent; and the crowds she had round her; and the things they *did*! Now, that was something, I can tell you, but Miss K. and Mr. P.! They weren't anything much. Miss K., once when she'd had a drop taken, she told me her ma wasn't even married. She'd been a kept woman." Mrs. Prosser spat out this last piece of information with such hatred, Hugo felt forced to protest:

"I thought you were fond of Mrs. Martyn?"

His comment was casual enough, but it brought Mrs. Prosser to an abrupt stop. She stood silent, fixing him with an unflinching stare, her nostrils inflated so that, with her long chin, she looked like an indignant orang-outang. "Well!" she burst out at last, "you're a nice one to cast aspersions, I must say. Sponging here where you're not wanted. I can tell you this: if it weren't for you, the Martyns wouldn't have to stay on here."

"Why? Where would they go?"

"Back to London, of course. What's to keep them here?"

"But I thought Mrs. Martyn had come here because of her brother and . . ."

"Couldn't she take him back with her?" said Mrs. Prosser. But now a note of uncertainty had come into her voice.

Hugo felt relief at it. She was, after all, speaking only from conjecture. He relaxed and stretched himself on the bed.

His gesture restored her annoyance and she said: "A lot of reason you've got to be so high and mighty!" She went, snorting, from the room.

Hugo turned disconsolately to the wall. He had been a fool to upset Mrs. Prosser, who was, if nothing else, someone to whom he could speak. He was also worried by her suggestion that but for him the Martyns could return to London. He did not want to believe it—and yet, why should they stay here? They were not Coldmouth people. They could do nothing here, and if Kyra could persuade Pippin to go with her, why should she stay? Surely London was the place for the Martyns? Both had lived and worked there before; they might find employment again.

Yet, wherever they went, Ridley would remain—a burden of rent, rates and upkeep! He tried to put Mrs. Prosser's remarks from his mind, but they persisted. He asked himself: If the Martyns wanted to leave Ridley, would he release them?

He did not know. He could no longer feel satisfaction in his position here. His defiance had failed him—yet, why should he call quits? He felt that by doing so he would admit defeat. Anyway, he would do nothing before he had drawn out and spent the last of his money and could present his case as he had not had a chance to present it before: "All right, I'll go—but I might as well tell you, I'm destitute."

But . . . it wouldn't do. He knew he could never say it. He must swallow his boredom and force Martyn to suggest an end; then he could agree: "I will go, of course, but . . ." He was not sure he wanted even the opportunity to say that.

At luncheon Mrs. Prosser had a viperish brightness. The meal was served. As her large, wrinkled hands, puffy as though continuously soaked in hot water, hovered over her knife and fork, she shuddered aggressively: "My goodness, it's cold in here!"

Kyra did not respond. It seemed as though the two women had quarrelled.

Mrs. Prosser went on: "With the winter on top of us, we ought to be ordering more boiler fuel. The last lot's running out quick."

"The price has gone up again," said Martyn.

"Perhaps it has, but you've got to have hot water. In a house like this you've got to have something hot."

Martyn's comment was a half sigh, a half puff of sheer exhaustion.

"If this place were mine," Mrs. Prosser continued remorselessly, "I'd close it up in the winter and go to a boarding-house. Boarding-houses are quite reasonable at this time of the year, but . . ." she turned her small, pinkish eyes on Hugo and gave him a baleful grin: "I suppose when you're burdened with dependents, you've got to stay put."

Martyn did not seem to catch the significance of this remark; he grumbled quietly: "Boarding-house, indeed! How do you suppose we could afford that?"

"It would be cheaper in the end."

"Nonsense," the headmaster cut her off irritably. "We'd still have Ridley. Don't be ridiculous, Mrs. Prosser."

Mrs. Prosser gave him an outraged stare: "I may be ridiculous," she said, "but I can tell you this: you're lucky to have someone to keep an eye out for you. I bet you don't know, for instance, that the ceiling's coming down in Classroom C?"

Martyn sighed, not wanting to know but in no position to repudiate knowledge.

"It'll be down on someone's head soon. And that won't be the only ceiling, either, I can tell you."

Martyn held up his hand. "I'll ring the builder this afternoon; but, in future, we will refrain from discussing the state of the house at meal-times. Our guest must be very bored by it."

The unusual firmness with which he spoke caused Mrs. Prosser to jerk up her head and stare at him in surprise. For several minutes words seemed to fail her, then, in a stage whisper of stagey contempt, she spoke once more. "Guest!" she said.

The rest of the meal was eaten in silence. Kyra left the room at the end of the first course.

"There's a pudding for afters," Mrs. Prosser shouted after her.

"I don't want any."

Mrs. Prosser collected the plates noisily together and went off to the kitchen. Hugo, left alone at the table with Martyn, thought: 'I could speak now. I could release him. I could say: "I'm going. I'm letting you off. You need not despise me any more," ' but he could not bring himself to the point of speech.

Martyn was a man in a position as desperate as Hugo's own; and in that position he behaved as Hugo would wish to behave. He behaved as Hugo might have behaved had he not struck enmity at the start.

But Hugo had struck enmity. As he thought of his money and all it had signified to him, he could not speak. Then Mrs. Prosser returned and the opportunity was lost.

A few days later Hugo drew out his last five pounds and closed his account. Coming so near to penury made him reckless. He took himself twice to a cinema during the week, and on Saturday night spent two hours in the Harbour Bar. He saw nothing of Kyra or Pippin.

During these days he felt an excitement of anticipation, for some reason certain this wretched situation could not imprison him much longer; though how it would end, or what he would do when it ended, he did not know.

The following Tuesday, with only a little more than

three pounds left of his money, he went down to the Row to make a tour of the public-houses. He had some idea of spending his every penny that evening, as though by achieving destitution he must hasten to some conclusion. He went to each of three small public-houses near the dockyard wall, then reached the Harbour Bar, which, on this night early in the week, was almost deserted. Soon he passed on to the small neighbouring public-house where he had met Kyra. She was there again. She looked up at his entry exactly as she had done before and recognised him with the same disappointment.

He said: "Still looking for Pippin?" She turned her head away without answering. He invited her to have a drink.

"No," she replied vaguely as though she had little idea what a drink was.

"I owe you one. What is that? Gin and French?"

She let him buy it. Her manner was disconsolate, and she made no attempt to talk.

He said: "What time were you meeting him?"

"Six."

The clock said quarter to ten. Hugo said: "I expect he'll drift in soon."

"I expect so."

Her gloom infected him, so they stood a long time dully silent. Then she spoke, affecting brightness: "Bumped into your girl friend yet?"

Hugo was bewildered a moment before he realised she meant Tilly. He replied: "It's not likely I will. The Webleys never had much contact with Coldmouth. She and Cyril would be more likely to drive to Brighton for an evening out."

187

"Oh! Cut above Coldmouth? What you might call county, eh?" She spoke in an exaggerated local accent. Hugo had no idea why she was ridiculing him; he could only keep quiet in fear of being ridiculed again. In the uncomfortable silence that followed he thought of making some excuse to go, but her look was so disconsolate he did not wish to leave her alone. The time dragged on. No one came or went.

The lights dipped and the barman called: "Last Orders," so, soon, there was no choice but to leave. Hugo supposed they would return together to Ridley, but when they got to the end of the Row Kyra paused at a side street.

"I must go round to my brother's lodging. He may be ill."

"Shall I come with you?"

She did not reply, but hurried off. He went after her, thinking any diversion better than none. They were in an alley that narrowed until the fog, hanging in the upper air, seemed compressed down on them in a grey, dank blanket full of graveyard cold. The discomfort made Hugo feel irritable and he said:

"Don't you think your brother can look after himself?"

"No." She was walking ahead. When they reached the road beyond and Hugo had room to catch her up, she added more gently: "Pippin is not only my brother, he's all that's left of the time when I had something to hope for. I was happy then—or I think I was. I don't know. I'm nothing now, anyway."

Hugo did not try to reply, not supposing that Kyra, any more than he, had belief in this past happiness. Judged from the present, anything might seem happiness, of course. He might even persuade himself there had been something pleasurable in those nights when he had returned home through these very streets after hours spent wandering companionless, moneyless, without object, putting time behind him until he knew his parents would have gone to bed. Even then there was one more ordeal to be endured. Each night as he passed his parents' bedroom door, his mother's voice would come quietly from the darkness:

"Is that you, Hugo?"

"Yes, Mother."

"Where have you been, dear?"

"Out with friends."

"Did you enjoy yourself?

"Yes, Mother."

"That's right. Good-night, dear."

"Good-night, Mother."

So, at last, to the safety of his room. He had felt maddened by her listening for his return. Surely when he spoke of his friends she must know he was lying. He felt a disgust with the whole process of question and answer, feeling it imposed on him to give her a vicarious sense of living. Her need to live through him had made him guilty. He felt himself failing her expectations, so that he had wanted to shout at her: 'Leave me in peace.'

Kyra, walking at a headlong pace, said: "I feel there's something wrong."

Hugo felt equally certain there was not, but he hurried with her. They were passing among old tenements where the street lamps, penetrating the fog, picked out corners of glistening, liver-coloured brickwork. Some windows were lit by the green-yellow of gas-light, but there was no living creature in the streets. It was not until they turned another corner that they found the idlers of the district concentrated round the entrance to a large building.

Kyra, nervously shrill, said: "Something has happened."

"Perhaps. But not to your brother."

She ignored his reply and hurried ahead. When they got to the large open doorway, she pushed through the crowd, saying sharply: "Excuse me. Excuse me," so that people automatically stood aside. They let her pass, but were careful neither to be pushed further into the hall nor to lose sight of what was to be seen inside.

Hugo recognised the building as the old Coldmouth Court-house that had been shut, with boarded windows, in his youth. Now, apparently, it had been converted to house the homeless. They entered a circular hall where two pillars of white marble, battered and filthy as far as the hand could reach, rose to the gilding of their untouched capitals. They supported a dirt-caked marble staircase beneath which a dozen dustbins stood in a row. Between the pillars the figure of a man was spread-eagled face downwards on a marble chequer-board floor. Set in the upper ceiling the remains of an immense chandelier lit the scene with two small yellow bulbs.

Kyra cried: "Pippin!" and ran forward, saying "I knew something had happened."

Hugo would have been glad to deny her certainty, but there was no mistaking the white, bone-thin curve of the nose visible through the film of ashen hair. He stood back, feeling nothing but a chilly shame that he had been so completely wrong in his reassurances.

The hall reeked of disinfectant. Pippin must have had a bottle in his pocket, for a pool of colourless liquid was soaking out from beneath his body. Its heavy smell almost disguised the stench of the dustbins beneath the stairs.

Kyra bent over the body a moment, her lips parted as though she might cry out again; instead she swung round and fixed her eyes on a man like a plucked chicken who was watching the scene from the stairs. She questioned him in an authoritative manner:

"What happened?"

"Fell down the well," the man answered hoarsely.

"But he's hurt. He's unconscious. Perhaps he's dead. Isn't anyone doing anything?"

" 'S'all right, miss; his mate's gone to telephone. Mustn't touch him till the cops come."

"But wasn't it an accident?"

"Couldn't say. Wasn't here when it happened. Better wait for the cops."

Kyra crossed to Hugo and said calmly: "I think he's dead."

"You'd better not touch him."

She stood, slightly bent, and said again: "He's dead. I think he's dead," then waited like everyone else for the arrival of police, doctor, ambulance or whatever was coming. As they stood in the rustling, whispering hall, Hugo became aware that more people were existing and breathing and watching silently from the landings above the hall.

"What's all this disinfectant?" he asked, suddenly.

Kyra said: "He always carried a bottle. He was afraid of . . . of infection."

A hand began sliding jerkily down the banister. A little old man moved out of shadow into the light that touched the grey stubble like a bloom on his cheeks. He made his way slowly down, moving his gums, and peering at the body with the bleak curiosity of a live dog looking at a dead dog. He muttered passionlessly:

"Broke his neck, has he? Poor old bugger."

As he neared the bottom of the stairs, he looked at Kyra and put on a pathetic air. "I want to go out," he said.

"No one's stopping you."

"He said not to leave the building."

"Who said?"

"His buddy."

"Do you know anything about the accident?"

"What, me?" quavered the old man indignantly. As he spoke, he hopped down the last step and, skirting the body in a wide arc, shuffled out quickly. Someone in the shadows above gave a cackle of laughter and was shussed by the rest; then there was a return to quiet until the sound of a car came down the street and stopped outside. There was a banging of car doors. Someone, talking loudly and excitedly, pushed a way through the crowd. It was Kinky Bluett:

"A thing like this is such a shock to the system," he was saying to the three, large, silent men who followed him. When he saw Kyra, he said: "My dear, you're here! Isn't it terrible? Isn't it *terrible?*" He gripped her arm excitedly.

"How did it happen?" she asked.

"I'm not sure. Not really sure." He released Kyra and smoothed back his hair, glancing over his shoulder with brilliant eyes. "I suppose you want a statement, officer?" he said, trying to talk in one way to Kyra and another to the policemen.

A sergeant stepped forward, lifted Pippin's eyelid and felt his pulse, then nodded to the others.

"Oh, I'm sure he's dead," Kinky agreed. "He fell right from the top floor. Such a shock! I can't tell you. I'd never been here before. I must say, I was surprised. I never thought he lived like this."

"Now, sir!" The sergeant spoke for the first time, his voice commanding an attentive silence all about him. "Perhaps you can give an account of what happened?"

"Dear me, yes. Well, it was like this, officer: Pippin was a little excited."

"Excited, was he?" The sergeant wrote something down. "Was anyone else present when the accident occurred?"

"Well!" Kinky's pause was a not unwilling betrayal.

"I must have full particulars, sir."

"Well, yes, officer, there was a young fellow, a very nice boy, but he had nothing to do with it."

"Where is he now?"

"He had to get back to his ship."

"His name, if you please."

"I've no idea. He said just to call him Jackie."

"I see. So you are of the opinion this young man's presence had excited the deceased?"

"Oh, no. I didn't say that. He was excited, but about something quite different. There'd been trouble with a man on that landing, a very nasty customer, a Mr. Gribbin. The council had put in a sink for all of them to use and this Mr. Gribbin wouldn't go down to the convenience on the second floor; he *would* use the sink. He said he had bladder trouble. Pippin didn't like it. He said the landing was smelling like a urinal, and so it was. Well, we'd just come in

193

and the door was still open, and Pippin heard someone on the landing and said: 'There's that old Mr. Gribbin again. It's too bad. I'm going to speak to him'. He went outside—and the next thing we knew, he'd toppled over."

"And what was this man Gribbin doing when the gentleman fell?"

"Nothing," screamed a thin, female voice from the top landing. "A nice thing bringing my old man into this. I knew we'd have something nasty happen with that sort in the house. No right to be living among decent people, I say. No one wanted him here."

"All right, madam," said the sergeant imperturbably, "we'll attend to you later." After he had questioned Kinky and discovered nothing more, he called upstairs for Mr. Gribbin to come down.

"He's gone out," shouted his wife. "The lady said for him to go."

Kinky looked accusingly at Kyra, who shrugged her shoulders. I'm sure it wasn't the old chap's fault. Pippin probably overbalanced. He's never been right since his last car crash."

Some ambulance men entered now. They lifted Pippin's body on to a stretcher, covered it and took it outside. At once the hall seemed empty. Doors opened and shut above as people returned to their rooms. The sergeant took the names and addresses of Kyra and Kinky, told them they would be required to attend the inquest, then dismissed them.

As they walked back to the Row, Kinky chattered happily: "What a terrible thing, darlings! I can't believe it. I *just* can't believe it. Pippin—dead! All in a minute. He just said: 'I'm going out to speak to him,' and then—*in a minute*—it was all over. I can't realise it, but I know I'll feel terrible when I do.''

Kyra did not speak. When they reached the Harbour, the Ridley bus was standing at the stop. Without a word she hurried to it as though she were alone. Hugo followed her and Kinky was left in the middle of sentence.

On the way back to Ridley, Kyra stared ahead of her with a stern, almost an angry, look on her face; she remained silent.

When they got off the bus at the end of the promenade the darkness hung like something tangible in the air. The wind was rising again. With a soughing monotony it swept off the black downland and struck their faces, harsh and icy as a wet sheet. Hugo could hear in the distance the uprise of the spray and the first winter booming of the waves against the undercliff.

Kyra walked ahead unfalteringly. Hugo, straining to see the glimmer of the path, kept finding himself impeded by grass. Suddenly the light was switched on in the hall at Ridley. It outlined Kyra plodding against the wind a few yards ahead of him. He hurried but could not catch her up before she entered the house. When he opened the door he saw Martyn standing under the hall light holding an evening paper in his hand. He was wearing his reading spectacles but Hugo felt this pretence at reading was merely a disguise. Martyn had been waiting for Kyra. As she passed him, he turned after her and Hugo heard him say:

"Kyra."

She must have murmured some response for he asked agitatedly: "What? What did you say?"

She ran upstairs and Martyn, throwing the paper aside, followed after her.

When Hugo passed their room, Kyra was saying: "I tell you, if he had been here it wouldn't have happened . . ." On his return from the bathroom, to which he had no more than pretended a visit, he heard Charles talking quietly. He paused, trying to hear something.

Kyra broke in on her husband: "You did it to destroy me. Whenever you've done anything, it's been to destroy me. This house, which you took behind my back . . ."

Martyn interrupted, raising his voice to be heard: "I took it to please you. You kept saying you must be with Pippin. You couldn't get word from him; you were making yourself ill with worry over him. I did not want to leave Scarborough. I came here solely for your sake."

"Whether you did or not, it was madness. To tie us to a dump like this! It was madness; absolute madness. Then to turn Pippin out! You bring me here because of him and then turn him out! What sense was there in that? What excuse can you give?"

"You know he was causing trouble here. He was a born trouble-maker. Worse than that. He'd got a hold on Brian. People were gossiping. Do you need any more excuse than that? How could we hope to survive with someone like Pippin in the school? I never meant that he should come to live here. If you hadn't brought him here everything would be all right now. My only lunacy was not turning him out straight away. I left it too late. When it came to a boy making a joke in class—well, what was I to do? What would you have done?"

Kyra made no attempt to answer that question; perhaps

she was not listening, but after a pause she said quietly and intently: "I should have gone with him. I might have saved him."

"You think he was worth saving?"

"He was my brother. He meant everything to me."

"And no one else meant anything?"

She did not reply. There was a long silence, and Hugo, afraid one of them would come out, had to leave the door and return to his room. In any case he had, he supposed, heard the basis of the argument. They would squabble a little longer with accusation and counter-accusation, then, each aware that nothing new was being said, they would go to bed.

Hugo went to bed himself. The room was grey with daybreak when he was awakened next morning by the sound of Kyra's departure. A door banged and opened again, then her voice poured past his room in a torrent of words and her heels rapped away down the stairs:

"You have been happy. You had those years with Patricia, damn her. I have never been happy. There must be something for me still. I'm going to find it . . ."

Martyn was following, calling: "Kyra. Come back." Hugo jumped out of bed and got the door ajar in time to hear Martyn, on the landing, saying quietly and urgently: "Don't leave me. I'm quite alone now."

Kyra, on the stairs, shouted back derisively: "What about your little girls? What about your memories—those bloody water-colours; that God-awful mauve dress!"

"For heaven's sake, Kyra, what will become of you? How will you manage alone? Surely you are not seriously thinking of the stage . . .?"

"Don't throw that up at me!" she was speaking from the hall.

"I'm not throwing anything up at you. I only want to get it clear what you have in mind. You can't just go off into the blue like this. What will you do?"

"Don't worry about me. My life's not ended yet. It's only beginning. I've been as good as dead here. . . . *Dead!*" The last word was a dramatic screech cut off by the bang of the front door.

In the sudden quiet that followed, Hugo tiptoed out to the landing. Martyn, his hands gripping the banister, was staring down at the door. He was dressed as he had been the night before. It seemed they had not been to bed.

Hugo stood still on the landing. Martyn moved to the stairs and had descended a few steps, slowly, when he crumpled and sat down as though too exhausted to remain upright.

On an impulse Hugo went to him and sat on the stair beside him. Martyn jerked his head round and, seeing Hugo, he flinched a little. "Excuse me," he said, "I . . . I'm a little faint." His words died in his throat, then, dropping his head into his hands, he whispered: "My wife has left me."

"Does it matter?" asked Hugo, who thought him well rid of her.

"Matter?" Martyn gazed down at the door, then round at Hugo with the hollow expression of someone in acute pain. Hugo was silenced, touched as he had never been before, by the long-suffering of a human creature.

Martyn said: "I must not keep you here in the cold. I'll go down to my study." He put one hand to the banister and drew himself up. "Thank you," he said, "it was good of

198

you," and he began in a laboured, cautious way to descend the stairs again.

Hugo said after him: "I wanted to tell you—if I can be of any help, I'll stay; but I'm willing to go whenever you wish."

Martyn stopped and, without turning, said: "It's not for me to say what you shall or shall not do. You have every right to stay here."

"I was not thinking of rights."

"I know; nevertheless, they exist." Martyn went on down the stairs.

Hugo watched him going, knowing he had no wish to talk now—but this opportunity might not come again. Hugo persisted: "I wanted you to understand: all that I said before didn't mean anything. I don't want to stay here. If it will help you, I'm prepared to go. If you could get rid of the house . . . or shut it up . . . or something."

Martyn, pausing again, said quietly, as though the matter were not of great importance: "The owner has offered to rescind the lease."

"No? You didn't tell me."

"I only heard a few days ago. The council wants the site for a housing estate. We might . . ." he laughed a little in spite of things, "we might even be offered some compensation."

"Of course you should be offered compensation." Hugo was eager and excited now, seeing the lease, that had been a burden before, become an asset, a saleable object that must not be filched from them.

Martyn nodded: "My solicitor will certainly bring that up. The money would go to you, of course." He made another attempt to continue to his study, but Hugo, stung now by the fear Martyn had supposed his only thought was for the money, stopped him again:

"You thought I behaved badly when you told me the school had failed. You've never spoken to me since— except when you couldn't help it. But I didn't mean to blame you. I knew you had done nothing dishonourable. I said what I did because I felt desperate. I didn't know what I was saying."

Martyn had reached the foot of the stairs. He made a slight movement of his shoulders as though adjusting himself to the need for this discussion, then he turned to Hugo and said: "We have misunderstood one another. I did not think you behaved badly. I thought it was you who did not wish to speak to me. I blamed myself. There was nothing I could do or say to mend matters. No suggestion I could make. I could only keep out of your way." He moved to the table and leant with his hand upon it. "You were so eager to come to Ridley," he said. "I imagined our working together to make a success of the school—but the school was done for before you even reached England. You were quite right to feel injured. And there was nothing I could do except hope that I might, one day, make good your loss. I still hope. There still seems to me a chance I shall hear from Brian, and once I'm in touch with him I may persuade him to return what is left of your money. I had a lot of influence over him once. I don't know what went wrong."

The light was strengthening. Martyn, lifting his head as he finished speaking, looked an old man. His face was grey with fatigue, and the mauvish skin beneath his eyes was heavily bagged. His arm trembled as he pressed it for support against the table. He sighed, looking down again, and said: "But my son is not my only failure. My wife thinks it is in my nature to let everyone down. She says my ineffectualness has ruined her life. She thinks the school would have collapsed in any case—just because it was my school. Perhaps she was right. I came here for her sake and she was wretched here. She thinks it is my fault Brian took the money. I deprived him of his friend, so he took the money. That is what she says. Pippin was to have joined him abroad somewhere. I don't understand. Brian could see Pippin in Coldmouth whenever he wished. I did not forbid it. What would have been the use? Who would have taken any notice of me? She even thinks that, indirectly, I was responsible for her brother's death. If I had let him stay here the accident would not have occurred. So she says. So she says. It may all be true. Perhaps you have more reason to blame me than any of them." Martyn spoke expressionlessly, without any hint either of vanity or self-pity, but as one prepared to face his own complete failure in life.

"This is nonsense," said Hugo. "You can't be blamed for everything . . ." but Martyn was not listening. He had started the journey across the hall to the study passage. Hugo did not try to stop him again, but watched him till he turned the corner, then went himself upstairs to his room.

It was too late to go back to bed. He dressed slowly, thinking with some satisfaction that now he was Martyn's only friend. Kyra and her brother—what had they ever done for Martyn? Kyra had weakened him with her discouragement. She had given him nothing. As for Brian— he was the worst of the lot. In his dealings with Pippin,

Brian had not had even the honour that is among thieves.

Outside the window a thread of sunlight, the first for a week or more, stretched across the grass. The spinney trees were bare. A few withered balls of roses still hung on the leafless rose bushes. Since his arrival here winter had stripped the garden, yet for the first time he looked at it without irritation. Its arrangement, he realised, was simple and in keeping with its size. When he looked in his shaving-glass his own reflection seemed to him equally satisfactory. While he shaved, he contemplated in his mind his new relationship with Martyn, imagining it as an extension of their first sympathy and a refuge such as each must need.

CHAPTER VII

WHEN Hugo went downstairs, hoping for breakfast, he saw Martyn going into the kitchen. He heard the kettle being filled. As the rush of water stopped, a key was turned in the front door and someone entered. At once Martyn, kettle in hand, face strained in anticipation, hurried out to the hall—but it was only the charwoman who came once a week to scrub the stairs and hall. Martyn's face fell as he saw her. She did not notice this, being herself full of news.

"What do you think," she cried, looking from Martyn to Hugo and back to Martyn, "there's been a train crash up the line. The boat train, they say. A head-on collision, hundreds of people killed."

"Where?" Martyn spoke, aghast.

She waved an arm: "Up the line. Between here and Crowhaven. A mile or two. My Bert's got a friend with a lorry. He picked up Bert and they've gone off to lend a hand."

"I must go, too." Martyn handed her the kettle.

"Oh, I wouldn't go," she said comfortably as she went into the kitchen, "there'll be plenty helping. Everyone enjoys a good smash-up."

Martyn went out by the back door. Hugo put on his own coat, which hung in the hall, and, taking Martyn's over his arm, ran after him. Martyn took his coat without comment. They passed together through the spinney up to the downs, where the grass was caked in frost.

Hugo could see a long way down the coast road. At a distant point, almost the point where the turning led down to the Webleys' house, there was a dark peppering of cars.

He said: "It's not far. About a mile."

Everything now looked different to him and nothing impossible. He felt excited at the thought he had excuse to go so near Tilly's home. Surely someone from the house would have gone to the crash to offer assistance! Perhaps she would be there herself. Perhaps, at last, the moment was coming when he would meet her face to face!

Martyn stared ahead short-sightedly and said: "Can you see the train? Can you see what has happened? I can't see anything myself."

No, there was nothing to be seen on the line.

"We must hurry," he said.

They got through the barbed-wire fencing and climbed up the steep bank to the rails. Martyn managed this without help. At the top he did not pause or glance round, but started along the track with a vigour Hugo would not have believed he possessed. Beyond the line the fields of yellowish earth were ridged, bare and chill. Over them lime was scattered like snow.

"Can you see anything now?" asked Martyn.

No. Ahead there was nothing to be seen but the glint of the naked rails converging in the distance. There was no noise except the occasional gritty crunch when one or other of them stepped off the sleepers. Suddenly the birdless, winter stillness was filled with the clang of a signal dropping over a side-line. Martyn gasped, but that was his only sign of agitation. The signal having dropped, the silence seemed deeper than before; then they began to feel something that was not yet sound but rather the first vibration of sound. The line began to drop toward Crowhaven, and Hugo could now see something in the distance. Trucks and people began to take shape and the noise became defined. A mile or so from the starting point they came upon the first spectators, several young men and a girl, standing about with sheepish half-smiles. Hugo and Martyn passed among them.

It was evident at once that the crash was a very minor affair. Hugo had expected the sort of spectacle he had seen on the screen: the overturned engine gushing steam; the carriages crumpled like matchwood—'matchwood' was the word; the scattered possessions of the dead and injured; but there was nothing like that. An engine had jumped the points and now two of its wheels were over the curve of the line so that it leaned like a lame horse. The carriages seemed intact. There was no sight of dead or injured—yet Martyn appeared no calmer. Hurrying to the first person with an official appearance, he breathlessly asked: "Please tell me: was anyone hurt?"

"No. No one." The man was writing in a note-book and did not look up.

"Where are the passengers?"

"There weren't any."

"So it wasn't the boat train?"

"No." The man sighed in consciousness of his own infinite patience. "The boat train went through ten minutes before this lot."

"Thank God!" Martyn stood a moment, then turned to Hugo and said apologetically: "I thought Kyra might have been in the crash."

"But why should she go to Crowhaven?"

"I thought she might be going to join Brian."

"I'm sure she doesn't know where he is."

"You think so? You really think so? She was speaking the truth, then?"

They were standing by the last of the half-dozen empty carriages that had been attached to the derailed engine. Martyn put out his hand as though he could not see properly what he sought to touch. Coming blindly upon the side of the carriage, he leant heavily against it. Gasping a little, he said: "Perhaps we should offer to help?"

"There is nothing we could do."

Hugo would have been willing to stand and stare a while with the others, but he could see Martyn was fit neither to stand nor to walk back to Ridley. He took his arm: "Better sit down; sit on the carriage step."

Martyn sat obediently; indeed he sank down as though it would not be in his power to resist. His hands dropped limply between his knees. He hung his head. Hugo noticed that his hands were shaking like the hands of a very old man.

The morning was clouding over. It was very cold. This was no place for Martyn to sit, yet, in this exhausted state, he could do nothing more. His unresisting collapse gave Hugo the sense of being in control. Consciousness of his own power filled him with something like tenderness for Martyn. He sat down beside him and put a hand on his arm. Martyn, raising his head a little, smiled.

"Excuse me," he said, "I'll be all right in a minute. Just a bit tired. Got no sleep last night."

"No hurry," said Hugo. "When you're rested we'll walk gently back."

Martyn nodded. After a while he said: "I'm sorry Kyra has not gone to Brian. It might have been the best thing for both of them. I suppose she's gone to London. She was always talking of making a 'come-back' on the stage, but I'm afraid she'll only fail again. She'd come to an end before I met her. She knew it then, but she forgot. Now she'll have to learn all over again. She doesn't learn easily. There's something gallant about her; about the line of her shoulders. Whatever she did, I could only feel sorry for her."

Hugo said nothing. He was thinking of himself as a man with the situation in his hands—a man dominant as men like 'Quids-in' and the other rugger players had been. The thought had about it a quality of delirium. It so raised his confidence, gave him such a sense of superiority over Martyn, that he was able to say:

"Even if we get some compensation for the Ridley lease, we'll have to find jobs. I like you. I'd like it if we could keep together. Perhaps we could work at the same school?" As he spoke he had no doubt things would happen as he wished them to happen. He would see that they did. Achievement seemed to him now simply a matter of his own will. "Do you agree?" he asked Martyn.

"Why not?" Martyn gave him a smile that was at once companionable and unbelieving, and Hugo, remembering it afterwards, realised his words must have been as remote to Martyn as the speech of an anæsthetist would be to a patient approaching unconsciousness, but as he spoke them, Hugo felt in himself something near elation. He was scarcely disturbed by the sight of his companion collapsing against the carriage door.

"What is the matter?" He asked prepared to put anything to rights.

Martyn did not reply. His eyes were closed. The official, who must have been watching from a distance, came over to them: "Gent overcome?"

"I'm afraid so. We'd been told the boat train was smashed up and people killed. He thought his wife might be in it."

"How do these stories get round? Lots of these people turned up expecting something sensational." The official lifted Martyn's chin with a competent and dispassionate hand. "Nervous collapse, I shouldn't wonder. Not a young man. Now, wait a mo." He crossed to the edge of the embankment and shouted down to someone on the road: "Here, you! Here's a job for you." When he returned, he said: "Lucky them fellows hadn't sheered off. They've been wanting a job."

Two young men climbed up the embankment and looked helplessly at Martyn. Were they, Hugo wondered, Bert and his lorry-driver friend?

"Now then!" said the official, and, working to his directions, they raised Martyn from the step. He opened his eyes to murmur: "Don't worry about me. I'll be all right."

"Where to?" asked one of the young men.

"Better take him to the Out-Patients for a check-up," said the official.

Martyn was half led, half carried down to the road and put into the front seat of the lorry. One man took the driver's seat, the other climbed into the back. The lorry drove off.

When it was out of sight, Hugo thought no more about Martyn.

For the first time since they had arrived on the scene, he was alone and free to look across the sea-coarsened, downland grass toward the Webleys' house. He had not been so near to it since his return. Now it stood a little to the right of him—there, on the cliff edge, not quarter of a mile away. A rough, flinty car track ran down to the gate. The trees at the front had become so tall and massed there was nothing to be seen now but the glimmer of the house front through the branches and the white cornice above them.

He remembered the dining-room that had been a-dazzle with sunlight when he played there, and full of the sweet, peppery scent of a rambler that grew round the french window. It seemed to him the small, yellow roses were still blooming there; that summer never left that room.

"Now," he told himself, "this is the time to visit her."

It was early; ten minutes past ten; not a conventional hour for paying calls, but what did that matter? Conventions meant nothing. He had the world in hand. He ran down the embankment and slipped between the wires with a movement of extraordinary ease. Anticipating their meeting with the delight of an indulgence, he considered what he would say to Tilly. The story he had to tell was no ordinary story: "Came to Ridley; found I'd lost everything. Saw the whole place breaking up; then understood I had to help. Somebody had to do something. It was for the younger and stronger to put things right. Now it's decided. We'll stick together; get rid of the house; get jobs at the same school. I'll arrange it all. Poor old Martyn'll need looking after."

Yes, that was the stuff to knock Tilly off her perch. Nothing else he could have told her could do the trick like a little heroism.

It was not until he was half a dozen yards from the house that he began to be aware something was wrong. The large iron gates were red-brown, not, as he had thought, with paint, but with rust.

As the last fifty yards took him up the rise to the high ground of the cliff head, he could see the gates were padlocked, but one was broken from its supports and hung askew so that anyone could enter round it. Hugo stepped through to a path bedded with black leaves.

The trees so hid the house that he had to pass beyond it before he could see its condition. He came to a standstill. The house had not been bombed. It had simply been abandoned. The windows were empty sockets. The façade's stucco had the look of crackle ware. In places the plaster had fallen showing the brick beneath. The summer picnickers had smashed the windows and forced open the front door. Through the door he could see the lathes of the hall ceiling fallen like a fan.

He felt no surprise; instead, as he looked about him, it seemed he recognised what he saw with that preternatural recognition of something once seen in a dream. Had he expected to find this? He was too benumbed to answer himself. He went on slowly, not certain he was not being watched. On either side of him the grass had been beaten down by rain, and the weight of autumnal leaves. There seemed to be a slight stir beneath it. He stopped; the noise stopped. It was followed by quiet the more disturbing because in it he felt himself emptied of intention.

Stone steps led up to the front door. The second step had fallen into the darkness of the cellar below. In the big, pillared porch, among dust and leaves and sodden newspapers, stood a single high-heeled shoe. On the step lay a bottle-rack someone had brought up from the wine-cellar, then found too cumbersome to carry further. Inside the hall, doubled back on itself with wool breaking through the ticking, was an old mattress, rain-swollen and very dirty.

When he entered the house, he could see that not only had the ceilings fallen but the roof, hidden from outside view by the cornice, was gone. He could look up through the broken ceiling to a sky as grey as slate. Of course, the roof had been removed so that the owner could avoid payment of rates. Hugo had heard of that before. So Cyril and Tilly had gone, wherever they had gone, with no intention of returning.

He moved cautiously across the hall, expecting the floor to collapse beneath him, but it remained firm enough. Nothing fell from above. In a corner lay a toy bucket painted with pictures of Donald Duck. Had Tilly had children? Or had this been left by an intruder child?

The sitting-room door stood open. Inside, the parquet floor had become a sea of static waves from the crests of which the wood blocks had sprung out to lie around in heaps like dominoes. He was afraid to cross it. He moved close to the wall, wanting to reach the great window, the famous window, that was now no more than space into which obtruded a spike or two of jagged glass. He came to the fireplace. Someone had made off with the surround, but the grate remained ready laid with age-yellowed paper and dusty coal, on top of which, with long beak and great eye-socket, was the skeleton of a bird.

He went on to the window space, passing three small, rusted radiators. A young tree had rooted itself in a corner of the window-sill, and now branched up taller than Hugo, half in the room and half out. He stepped over the sill to the wrought-iron balcony and looked down upon a lawn of bramble and docken. Beyond was the wintry sea. The cliff had broken away, taking with it part of the garden wall. An old fig tree that had grown against it now clung to the cliff edge by bare roots, its branches, like grey-silver wicker-work, hung with small figs. A net of creeper, stretching itself over the garden, seemed to quiver as though a world of life were hidden beneath it—yet, when he watched it, he saw there was no life; nothing moved. The place was in its desolate, winter death. There was nothing to be heard but the steady shush of the waves breaking at the cliff's foot.

It seemed to him scarcely believable that all the time he had imagined Tilly living here in warm and lighted rooms there had been no human life at all—nothing but wind and rain and cold beneath the forlorn cover of the rafters. He wondered when the house had been evacuated. For how many years had the skeleton bird lain on the hearth as on a bier? And where was Tilly? He did not know. It was more than likely the Webleys had left Coldmouth altogether. She might not even be alive. The house and Coldmouth, and, indeed, the world, seemed now an emptiness about him.

Where could he go from here? He felt completely lost. Gazing about him like a sleep-walker awakened suddenly in an unknown place, he was bewildered by the scene he saw. How was it his life had done nothing more for him than bring him to the ruin of this house? Whether he turned to past or future, he seemed to turn to an equal emptiness.

Well, he could not stay here. He made his way from the room to the hall. When he saw the curving staircase with its elaborate banister, he remembered Webley again. . . . That must be the banister over which Cyril and his envied companion had watched the dinner guests descend. Well, anyone could descend now. He might as well go down. Under a litter of glass chips and fallen plaster, the stair was firm—a stone staircase, an expensive staircase. It turned at the bottom, so he could see it was still supported by Italianate pillars, each twisted like a sugar stick.

As he went down, the dining-room came into view—a long room made gloomy by the creeper curtaining the windows. Cyril's best friend, Stripe, once said of it: "It's a hundred per cent spiffing. Just like a room in a film." Now the great expanse of the floor sank basin-deep in the middle, and the ceiling over it sagged like a tarpaulin. Someone had wrenched out the radiators, then rejected them. They lay rusted among heaps of dust and rubbish and blown-in leaves. The rambler, become a tangle of briar, blocked the space that had once been a glass door.

Hugo, stepping down to room level, realised that one of the dark patches on the floor was a human figure. It sprawled with the abandoned stillness of the dead. The body of a tramp dead of exposure?—yet, perhaps, not dead? His first impulse was to hurry off before the man should see him; then, caught both in curiosity and compassion, he felt impelled to go to him. He kept near the wall and arrived safely beside the body. As he bent over it, he was assailed by its aura of decay. He retreated at once. Skirting it widely, he came to the doorway, where he could stand in a stream of fresh air and look without nausea. The face was hidden beneath an outstretched arm; the hand, which lay toward him, light-coloured and delicate, was not the hand of a tramp. On the further side there was a small suitcase that had been tipped open. Keeping between the body and the windows, he went close enough to see, among a drift of leaves, a shirt, a couple of ties, a pair of lavender socks rolled in a ball, a razor, soap and towel. Within the curve of the right arm lay some sort of book. He snatched it up and retreated again. It was a child's exercise book labelled *Ridley House School*. He opened it. On the first page was scrawled in pencil:

'Had a smash. Tried to get back. Leg broken. I think something wrong inside. Finished up here.'

Beneath this the same hand, grown laxer, had added:

'In case this is curtains, regret everything. Knew I'd been a B.F. as soon as I got away from her.'

Last of all, barely legible, the words straggling down the page:

'Still awaiting message from the outside world.'

'As soon as I got away from her . . .'—the pronoun struck Hugo oddly. In his conjectures the story had been different. Not that that mattered?—and yet he felt, suddenly, extraordinarily deprived, as though in the whole of his life, an

element had eluded him without which he could understand nothing. Surveying the history of his return, he ended on Charles Martyn's last smile as on a point of revelation. He knew now it was not Martyn who had been the simpleton. Martyn, smiling, had humoured him as if to say: "Of course, if you want to play at being 'Quids-in' and those other heroes, by all means play." Yes, it was all one to Martyn then. Hugo could not resolve his life by following Martyn, who had grown over-tolerant and was too near the end.

He read the last sentence again, reflecting that this humour in extremity was the only sight he would ever get of Brian Martyn's character, then he turned the page and found, interleaving the book, a sheet of paper, white and fine as rice paper—a five-pound note. Then another and another. Running the pages through his fingers, he saw between them note after note.

His money. Probably all of it. To do with as he liked! Yet, as he took the first note from the book, he felt guilt as though the dead man had been his victim. The sensation was beyond his comprehension. Who had been robbed? Who deprived by circumstances? Who victim?—if not he.

As for *guilt*! The word caught at him oddly as though it should have more meaning than he would admit. With an exasperated movement he returned the note to its original place, then flung the book back to the corpse. That, anyway, was a matter for the police. The money had lain there safely since Brian's death, it could lie a little longer. It would be returned to him some time.

He hurried upstairs and out of the house, but his escape

did not restore him. He supposed the discovery of the body had disturbed him more than he knew. He waited for the open air to smooth him like a sedative; instead his irritation grew. He was oddly stirred by the smell of the garden's wet and rotting vegetation. It transported him to Menteh, to the side of the Nile that at evening gave off this dank and grey-green smell. For a moment time and country changed for him. He saw Abdul's eager and significant glance across the rickety table.

"They all mistook me," he said, "I am another person," and impatiently he shook off the Egyptian air and trampled his way out through the dead English leaves.

Why, he asked himself, have I been so pestered by the past? For now all his confidence had failed; he was no longer a man in the right.

He hurried to get away from the garden. He was frightened by the unfamiliarity of his own reactions. It was as though some piece of the mechanism of his mind no longer responded to his direction. Something had been going wrong since his return to Coldmouth. Returning he had found—nothing. Well, if his past were so extinguished, what had he lost? Little more than the repository of his grievance. A loss, perhaps; it had been, if nothing else, an armour against reality. Now he felt like a child in the world; at the beginning again. Or had he never set out at all?

With an intense and increasing irritation he began to feel he was being cornered into admitting that in all his life he had not advanced a step. Yet, if the circumstances of his past had forced him into a prison of resentment, why should he feel guilt?

He said to himself: 'Too much has been imposed on

216

me;' and there came over him the same anger he had known when Martyn told him his money was lost. Yet even this anger had an unfamiliar sting. Turning upon it as it gained on him, he recognised it for what it was—another aspect of his own guilt.

He was out of the garden now. Without looking again at the house, he followed the wall round to the cliff edge. From here a path crossed the downs to Ridley. All the morning's brightness had gone. The sky was darker than the sea. There was a pin-pricking of rain in the air. The sea's surface was peaked and plucked and feathered by a rising gale.

As he set out on the path, the wind swept through the trees behind him and, entering the abandoned house, slammed one of its doors. The report that reached him was like a decisive slam of fact upon his life's defence. He felt himself thrust out. Condemned. It seemed to him he had understood nothing and he did not know what he was required to understand. Yet, even as he touched despair, his mood changed. If he were guilty, then he himself, not circumstance, had been his depriver. His life had always been in his own hands. It was in his hands now—but what was he to do with it? Facing his own liberation, he almost wished again for the resentment that had blocked every path for him. Now he must accept responsibility. Now there was nothing he could not do.

When Ridley came in sight, he thought: 'I will see Charles Martyn again, but not now. I must solve my own problem first.'

Nothing was clear to him. He knew only he had struck at last against some reality he had evaded all his life. Thinking of those who had seemed to demand of him more than he had ever thought to give, he wondered if they held a glimmer of solution. Had he always been a stranger in the world, not understanding its main language, unable to answer anyone who spoke it to him? If so, his ignorance had been a perverse ignorance. Understanding had been within his reach and he had refused it. Those who had approached him—had they known more of him than he had chosen to know of himself? And, failing them, had he failed himself? He did not know. He knew only that he was a person other than the one for whom he had mistaken himself. What he was, he had still to discover.

When he reached the edge of the downs he was, from habit, about to turn and look back at the Webleys' house when he remembered and did not turn. There was nothing behind him now. The accoutrements of his past had all dwindled like objects in time's landscape that was itself no more than a toy in relation to eternity. He knew now those details that had possessed him were like the monstrous up-shouldering of memory that in Menteh had made him weep in self-pity at Tilly's cruelty. They had meant no more than that. As they faded from him, a few faces remained substantial in his mind. Pausing for the last time beneath the spinney trees, glancing over those who endured for him, he reached with regret that last sight of Martyn. In the past, lacking the language of response, he had made his partings with relief at escape from relationships always unsatisfactory. What he had now to give, he did not know, but told himself: 'I will meet Martyn again,' then he stepped out from the safety of the trees.

He had no choice but to advance and discover. The past

by disintegrating beneath his feet had forced him to move on to unknown territory. He had lost the security of injury. Now there was no excuse.

How long this mood would last he did not know, but he felt he must make a decisive step while he could draw upon the strength of it. He reached the house and went straight to his room. Most of his cases were still unpacked. He packed the rest and took them all down to the hall. He stacked the larger ones in a corner and kept only the one he had brought with him. Mrs. Prosser was in the kitchen. He told her how they had gone to the scene of the rail accident, how Martyn had collapsed and been taken to hospital. She showed no great interest but, looking at the suitcase in his hand, asked with interest: "You off? Where are you going?"

"I'm not sure. Please ask Mr. Martyn if he'll keep that luggage for me. I'll send for it some time. And tell him—he'll understand—that he owes me nothing. I don't want anything."

The ironical glint in Mrs. Prosser's eyes implied that in her opinion it would be all the same if he did.

'That's all you know,' Hugo thought as he turned to leave.

"But where will we forward your letters?" Mrs. Prosser followed him to the door.

"I don't get letters. You know that. Good-bye." He closed the door on further questions and set off across the grounds.

At the pier end of the promenade he left the bus and walked through to the police station, where he reported his finding of Brian's body. He gave his address as Ridley House School; then, with the sense of having closed a circle and left himself outside it, he walked on to the Harbour Station. He bought himself a single ticket to London. That left him with sixteen shillings, a credit balance with which to encounter the world.